Praise for *Cheval*

"Terry Hetherington was a wr[...]
lived with a spirit of generosity for others. He would have
been delighted and proud of the influence the award set up
in his name has had on the career of writers in Wales, offering
opportunity and recognition."
Richard Lewis Davies, publisher

"More than anything, winning the Terry Hetherington award
rooted me in a community of writers… The prize paved the
way for publications, bursaries, mentorships and awards that
may not have come to fruition without that first winning
short story." **Mari Ellis Dunning**

"Winning a Terry Hetherington Young Writers Award put my
poetry on the map. It gave me the chance to meet other young
writers in Wales, speak to Welsh publishers, and join a
respected network of previous award winners. I am so
grateful for the ongoing support from the Cheval Trust and
look forward to reading the anthology every year."
Christina Thatcher

"The Terry Hetherington Competition was the first writing
competition I entered so I was over the moon to win 2nd
prize… twice, keeping company with future international
prize-winning writers. Each year the enthusiasm that the
Cheval group shows in encouraging & fostering a bounty of
creative youth is bound between these pages where poets,
storytellers, but most importantly writers of all kinds, find
their words are given a voice to speak of Wales' young talent."
Siôn Tomos Owen

"Being a finalist for the Terry Hetherington award was a real
milestone for me. It gave me confidence in my writing and
also encouraged me to take my work in new directions. I'm

still in touch with other writers and industry professionals I met at the ceremony. It's an excellent opportunity for up-and-coming writers and long may it continue." **Tyler Keevil**

"The Terry Hetherington Award is a valuable springboard for fledgling writers beginning to navigate the dense thickets of showcasing and publishing their work. The organisers are warm, enthusiastic and welcoming gatekeepers of the Welsh writing community." **Eleanor Howe**

"The support of Aida and the Terry Hetherington team proved more than just a one-off opportunity – I've made lifelong friends and felt supported from that very first entry to my third published book. Honoured to be involved with it today – a vital fund for young writers in Wales."
Natalie Ann Holborow

"Winning this prize just under a decade ago helped me believe in myself. Would I be a freelance writer today without it? I'm not sure." **Lowri Llewelyn**

"The Cheval anthology is one of my favourite reads every year. It's always been such an honour to be included! Over the years, the feedback has given me so much confidence but also helped me improve." **Nathan Munday**

"I don't think I would have been any sort of writer at all without *Cheval*. Recognition came from the Terry Hetherington Award at a time when I could quite easily have given up, and I am so grateful for the confidence and belief in my work the award gave me. When one looks at the list of writers the award has fostered, it's true to say that we have a generation of writers in Wales that this award has helped bring to prominence. This is all down to the volunteers who work tirelessly in supporting this award. Endless applause to them, and all great power to *Cheval*!" **Jonathan Edwards**

Natalie Ann Holborow is the multi award-winning Welsh writer whose debut collection, *And Suddenly You Find Yourself* was listed as one of Wales Arts Reviews 'Best of 2017' and was launched at the International Kolkata Literary Festival. She is a finalist for the Cursed Murphy International Spoken Word award and a curator for Taz Rahman's 'Just Another Poet' project, a virtual poetry exchange showcasing work from Wales and across different cultures worldwide. Her second collection, *Small*, is out now.

Molly Holborn is an author and student currently living in Llanelli. She published her first children's book in October 2019, and since then has been studying an MSc in Marketing at Swansea University. This is her second year editing the *Cheval* anthology. Molly is also working on a novel which she hopes to publish by the end of 2020 inspired by one of her favourite Greek goddesses. When she is not writing or reading, you'll find her walking or cycling along the Millennium Coastal Path with her partner and her loving canine sidekick, Nala.

Also available

Cheval 13

Edited by Molly Holborn
and Natalie Ann Holborow

Foreword by Aida Birch

PARTHIAN

Parthian, Cardigan SA43 1ED
www.parthianbooks.com
Print ISBN 978-1-912681-86-0
Ebook ISBN 978-1-912681-99-0
First published in 2020 © the contributors
Edited by Natalie Ann Holborow and Molly Holborn
Cover Design by Emily Courdelle
Typeset by Elaine Sharples www.typesetter.org.uk
Printed by 4edge Limited

Contents

Foreword

Terry Hetherington, my late partner, was a widely published poet. His fuller enjoyment of creative writing experience was by encouraging young people to write. The validity of the Terry Hetherington Young Writers Award is by responding sensitively to every entry.

The identity of the contributor is not revealed until judging is completed. It is rewarding to see new young writers, as well as young writers who have appeared in the pages of previous *Cheval* anthologies. The 2020 prize winner is Rhodri Diaz. He has had stories published in previous *Cheval* anthologies. His prize-winning story, 'The Bones of You', is a realistic story that includes a sense of place. Cwmgwrach is a little village in the Neath Valley, sometimes called 'The Valley of the Witch'.

Nathan Munday's poem '23rd of October', awarded 2nd Prize for Poetry, has a grim reality: 'but a vessel of death in the form of a truck'. A poem without a romantic illusion but words that record 'a vessel of death'.

Second Prize for fiction, 'Preiddeu Annwn', is an absorbing story by Cara Cullen. Cara has a gift for character intervention and has a lively eye for dramatic incidents. The author creates the main character; 'a rain soaked walker covered in mud'. The passenger on the train that the walker meets is a woman with three little dogs.

The highly commended prize for fiction is by Gareth Smith titled 'Mam', but is she really a Mam? Gareth has stories published in previous anthologies, and he has a great skill for character invention.

The essential task of the judges for the award is to uncover contributors' talent for creative writing. *Cheval 13* provides readers with illuminating poetry and fiction. Many previous prize-winners are now published poets, others are fiction writers. One of the editors of *Cheval 13*, Natalie Ann Holborow, has become a widely published poet, with her second full collection due out this year.

Aida Birch

Preface

by Natalie Ann Holborow

The Terry Hetherington Young Writers Award has long been an esteemed and vital platform for young writers living and writing in Wales, and one that many of today's published Welsh writers can attribute as the start of their literary careers. Both Molly and I know only too well how important it is that young writers are supported in their creative endeavours in a world where writing and publishing can feel so full of rejection and knockbacks. *Cheval* is a celebration of young talent from all walks of life, one which previous editor and award-winning poet Jonathan Edwards once noted is full of love: 'love that the judges and organisers bear for young people and for the man for whom this award is named', 'love of these young writers for language', and the love that young writers clearly have for their readers. This he noted in 2012.

Now, in 2020, that love has never felt more apparent, nor indeed necessary in this world we are currently living in.

Cheval 13 offers up a plenitude of themes and subjects: angels and demons were aplenty (this bore a remarkable resonance: good versus evil feels startlingly relevant), with Jonathan Macho's 'Wrong Number' presenting the subject with a wry wit that wouldn't look out of place in a Terry Pratchett novel. By the end of his story I found myself unexpectedly uplifted by the tale of the Upper Cwmtwrch Satanist Society. Who'd have thought?

Family remains a strong theme this year, with second-place prize winner Nathan Munday's poem 'Death of Tadcu Preacher' a heart-rending tribute to the man whose 'hair waved across his head. This wet ocean. This stinging salt.' The emotional gravity with which Munday delivers his poem makes a standout contribution in his poem '23rd of October', telling of an incident where Essex police had discovered thirty-eight adults and a teenager who had passed away in a Bulgarian truck: '...blood-stained lands / where big dogs bark in Westminsters. / There is no policy candle which can switch / their eyes back on.'

Cara Cullen's 'Preiddeu Annwn' is an example of tenderly-written fiction, deserving of being a prizewinner alongside Nathan Munday's, with a sharp observational eye that verges on the poetic: 'She had three fat, breathless little dogs waddling under the table. I could see their heads move in and out of the shadow around her feet like a seething pile of wrinkled flesh.' Again, bonds link back to family, this time not the Welsh 'tadcu' but a grandfather of Irish descent. I found myself smiling at the reference to the Book of Kells, something which I too was enchanted by whilst once visiting Trinity College in Dublin.

First-place prize winner Rhodri Diaz is a familiar name in the *Cheval* anthologies and for good reason. His story, 'The Bones of You', has all the magic of a Welsh folk tale, delivered in the form of a highly readable and beautifully written piece of short fiction. Linking also to Welshness, and the power struggle between good and evil, he writes: 'I used to think that there was no evil that couldn't be defeated if we only tried hard enough, but that isn't true. Some evil grabs hold and refuses to let go, no matter how much you beg and pray and cry. Some evil burrows and takes root in the very marrow of you, and rots you from the inside out. Some monsters simply can't be slain.' How very true.

Jannat Ahmed brings a refreshing voice to the poetry scene in Wales with 'Essence', experimenting with form and language with a confidence that fizzes: '*pungent* with *desire* to bend, break, blow, burn a language new / unscented with the body / of work and millennia'. Meanwhile, Sophie Evans's 'Losing Touch' offers a heartbreaking story of a mother's yearning for her lost child, written with piercing skill: 'He sighed and the doors hissed shut. I looked back over at the lady beside me. She sat there on the pale red bench of the shelter with surprising elegance, smugly holding her rounded tummy. A gust of wind blew through the gap of the shelter, ruffling the tops of our head but the hank of her ponytail remained unmoved. Next to her, a little girl with matching copper hair neatly weaved into a French plait.'

Cheval 13 is a journey. It's a journey out of, and back home again, to Wales. It's an exciting showcase of the most exciting fresh voices in Welsh literature today and you're in for an eye-opening ride. Times are challenging, but these young voices are roaring out of the darkness.

Buckle up. Listen. Be inspired.

Natalie Ann Holborow

Preface

by Molly Holborn

2020 has been a string of uncertainty and anxiety, but what is certain is when times are dire creativity remains strong and fierce. Reading and editing through the entries of this year's *Cheval* anthology has been an utter pleasure. To see the variety in imagination has proven that poetry and prose are a necessity to thrive in the world today.

Cheval 13 has shown a multitude of powerful themes and language. From a witch in Cwmgwrach, the catastrophe on October 23rd, and a mysterious gold coin, the entries this year have taken both the fictional and the non-fictional and weaved tales of immense emotion and power that prove the effect of the written word. The theme of good and evil is one that has stood out this year, more specifically how everything is not always as it seems. Characters that you think you know or stories that you think you can predict are something else entirely. Like in winner Rhodri Diaz's 'The Bones of You', a story much like Celtic folklore that shows you the vicious cycle of good and evil that never truly ends, his story was beautifully self-contained and easy to read whilst still being so provoking.

Much like Cara Cullen's 'Preiddeu Annwn', Gareth Smith's 'Mam' has that anxiety similar to that of a fight or flight situation: your mind is telling you that something is very wrong but the environment itself is still, like the calm before the storm. That type of writing has left me feeling nervous but also extremely impressed because isn't that what writers do? They leave us feeling what they intended way after that final full stop.

As well as the stories, the poetry has been just as thought provoking. Nathan Munday's '23rd of October' was utterly breathtaking, it takes a very real and serious event and gives a voice to those who perished and for that, it was an honour to read. In a completely different way, Emily Hancox's 'Aberdulais Bwbach' gives a sense of nostalgia when reading it, reminding those of us who grew up with tales of Welsh myths of their roots in a beautiful child-like way, again such powerful emotion. It made you feel proud to be Welsh, to give a memory that you thought you had forgotten and that is priceless.

I could write an anthology in responses to every single entry I read for *Cheval 13* but I have a message that links to you all: you have put a piece of yourself into the world, a fierce and creative force that allows others to escape without having to move at all. The readers will thank you, though you won't hear it; you will inspire other writers, though you may not know it. But know that you are the wonderfully talented writers and poets of Wales; keep writing and keep dreaming.

To all the *Cheval* team, I thank you for another year with the anthology. It has been an absolute pleasure, and to Aida Birch, who welcomed me into her home and sent the most heartwarming of emails, thank you.

To Natalie Holborow, who has been the best co-editor and friend, I thank you for all your help and support, I truly appreciate it. As well as the continued encouragement when life gets tough. Here's to more coffee dates!

All my love and take care,

Molly Holborn

Terry Hetherington

Seagull over Neath Marsh

A glorious early Sunday morn,
I walked the springy marshland grass,
Without a living soul in sight,
How languidly the time slipped past,
The Nedd swelled gently with the tide,
and pushed her flotsam to the side,
The world stood still, I cast my gaze
Up to a golden glimmering haze,
And saw on high in lonely flight,
A solitary seagull white,
His slender pinions rode the air
Just he and I the world to share,
It seemed, when from the rivers edge
concealed till now by sun warmed sedge,
Like some gigantic morn trapped ghost,
There rose a screaming, squabbling host,
Who, heading for the distant sea
left the world once more to me.

First Prize

Rhodri Diaz

The Bones of You

I can remember exactly where I was when I first heard about the witch of Cwmgwrach. Among schoolchildren, whispers spread like wildfire and our chief spymaster was Little Tomos Charles. He was, you might have guessed, a diminutive lad with a permanent smirk plastered across his face and beady eyes that followed you around the room. If he had no other talents, he would have been thoroughly unlikeable, but he quickly became our primary source for tall tales and urban legends. He managed to convince us one summer that dialing 666 on the village phone box would cause the Devil to pick up, and he insisted up to his dying breath that his father worked for MI5. It was Little Tomos Charles who first told us about the Witch of Cwmgwrach. He liked to hold court at break-times, sitting on a wooden stool in the middle of the classroom while the rest of us sat around him in a semi-circle as he spun his latest yarn.

'She lives in a little hut in the middle of the woods. You know it's her house because there's a broom outside, like. If the broom is standing up, she's in. If it's lying on the floor, she's out. She's lived there for five hundred years, so I'm told. She can do all sorts. Make up potions, turn people into frogs, anything you fancy really.'

Undeterred by our snorts of derision, he carried on, 'Cwmgwrach, bois. Cwm. Gwrach. It means Valley of the Witch. You can't call a place that without good reason. It's false advertising. I'm telling you, she's real.'

'Can she heal people?' I asked.

'Eh? What you on about?'

'Can she make people better? If they're not well and that,' I said quietly.

Little Tomos Charles furrowed his brow. 'I dunno. Aye, probably. She can do most things. You wouldn't want to ask her though.'

'Why not?' I asked.

'Snatches kids, don't she. Puts them in a pot and cooks them in a stew for her tea.'

Not long after, my father sat me down one evening after school and told me that there was nothing more the doctors could do for Mam. I'd come bounding through the door and gone straight to the kitchen to pour a glass of pop. I knew that something was wrong when Dad didn't chide me for 'drinking that muck' as he usually did. He just sat on the sofa, still as a statue, staring into space with a glassy-eyed expression. Dad had one of those faces, weathered, wrinkled and pock-marked, that you only see in black and white photographs. A face that seemed alive with adventure and stories, and a life lived. He was an old-fashioned man, of ancient mining stock, with hands like shovels and a truly monstrous moustache. If you cut him, he would have bled coal dust and bitter ale. I'm telling you all this so you understand exactly how remarkable it was when, after telling me that Mam had about six months to live, my father held me tighter than he ever had before and wept until his eyes were raw. I didn't cry. Not then, at least. I can only recall a gnawing ache in the pit of my stomach, and wanting nothing more than to climb to the peak of the tallest mountain in the world and scream until my lungs burst. I can only remember feeling like a shattered piece of porcelain, desperately trying to piece myself together again before the next blow fell.

Some parts of this story I remember clear as day, and some parts are murkier, harder to picture, like I'm looking at them through frosted glass. It's been fifty years since it all happened, and it seems that for every wrinkle my face gains, a part of my memory fades.

Here are some of the things I do remember: I remember that we still lived in the old tumbledown cottage that had once been my great-grandfather's pride and joy. He had built it by hand, and it showed. My father used to say that one short, sharp shove would send the whole thing tumbling to the ground, but whenever my mother would suggest selling up and moving elsewhere, his face would tighten and he would say 'No, not now, *bach*. The boy is settled.' I remember that I was gangly and awkward, with a few wispy hairs on my upper lip and a voice that crackled like radio static, the only indicators that I was about to be thrust unwillingly into manhood. And I remember what my mother looked like after cancer had spread to her bones. Pale and brittle, as if she would break into a thousand pieces at the slightest touch. She reminded me of that thin paper that old Bibles used to be printed on.

I used to think that there was no evil that couldn't be defeated if we only tried hard enough, but that isn't true. Some evil grabs hold and refuses to let go, no matter how much you beg and pray and cry. Some evil burrows and takes root in the very marrow of you, rotting you from the inside out. Some monsters simply can't be slain.

After we got the news, I was allowed a few days off school, which I mostly spent lying on my bed, staring at the ceiling and trying to imagine a life without my mother in it. It was as I lay there, basking in the late-autumn sunlight that streamed through my bedroom window, that I remembered Little Tomos Charles and his far-fetched story. Under normal circumstances, I would never have entertained the idea of trying to find a witch, but whenever I thought about my mother, about her Sunday dinners and the way she would pretend not to laugh at my antics when Dad was around and the way her skin smelled when she held me close, it felt as if my heart was being torn from my body. Mam was life, and life was Mam, and separating the two was like asking someone to give up their shadow.

A plan began to formulate in my mind. I would find the witch's house, nestled deep in a copse of trees. I would walk through the rickety gate, past a garden overgrown with weeds and tangled vines, and knock on the door. It would open with a creak and a bony finger would poke out, beckoning me inside. I would step into a gloomy porch reeking of incense and old blood. The witch, hunched and covered in warts and boils, would ask in a voice like shattered glass 'What can I do for you, my child?' and I would ask her to save my Mam. The witch would brew a glimmering green potion in her pewter cauldron and I would take it home to pour in Mam's tea and we would live happily ever after in our ramshackle cottage and the word "cancer" would be banished from the realm forever.

That's not what happened. This is not a fairytale.

*

The next morning, after Dad had gone to work, I made myself a round of corned beef sandwiches and a flask of tea, stowed them in my rucksack and set out without much of an idea

5

where I was going. The ground outside was covered in a thick carpet of crisp caramel leaves and my every step was accompanied by a satisfying crunch. After an hour of walking, and a brief pit stop to polish off my sandwiches, I arrived at Cwmgwrach. It was, to my surprise, not a dense and moody patch of woodland but a village, unremarkable and plain. I walked up and down the rows of terraced houses, trying desperately to find one that had a broomstick or an overgrown garden until my feet stung and the straps of my rucksack cut into my shoulders. I began to feel utterly lost. My eyes started to burn and before I could stop it, the dam broke. I collapsed to the floor, weeping and beating my fists against the pavement. After a few minutes of this, my knuckles raw and stinging, I sensed a presence. An old woman was staring at me from the porch of a nearby house. She was squat, with a plump and kindly face, grey hair set into a perm and prescription spectacles.

'You alright there, love?' she shouted.

'Are you the witch?' I said before I could stop myself.

'Is that what they're calling me these days? Come inside, love. We'll get those hands looked at.'

I pulled myself to my feet clumsily and shuffled towards the woman, who ferried me through the door. Her house was cosy and filled with knick-knacks and bric-a-brac from floor to ceiling. I was shown into the kitchen, where I sat at the table as the woman applied antiseptic cream to my knuckles. A pot of cawl was bubbling away on the stove, the aroma enveloping me like a warm hug. After my wounds had been dressed, the woman poured me a cup of steaming hot tea and served up a slab of bara brith, still warm from the oven, spread with a thick layer of salty butter. It was, after nothing but dry corned beef sandwiches all day, the most wonderful thing I'd ever eaten.

'Scuse me,' I said through a mouthful of cake, 'what's your name?'

'Annie,' said the woman. 'And yours?'

'Harry.'

'Well, Harry,' she said, 'are you going to tell me why you were beating seven bells out of my pavement?' Her voice was gentle and musical, and any notion I might have had of lying to her was washed away by her soothing tone.

'One of my pals told me that a witch lives around here,' I said, realising with every word how stupid and childish I sounded.

Annie chuckled softly. 'There's a few around here who deserve to be called that, but I can't say I know of any real witches. What do you want a witch for anyway?'

'My mother. She's not well. She's…' I tried to speak, but the words stuck in my throat and my eyes started to sting again.

'And you thought this witch could help your mam, is that right?'

I nodded. Annie tapped my hand affectionately, got up and took a picture off the mantelpiece. It was of a young man in an army uniform, with slicked-back hair and a jaw you could sharpen a knife on.

'That's my Andrew, that is. It's his birthday today. The cawl's for him.'

'Oh, then don't let me keep you, I'll…'

For the first time, I noticed a piece of paper, yellowing and frayed at the edges, sitting on the tabletop. From my vantage point, I could only make out a few brief sentences. 'Dear Mrs. Parry, it is with the deepest regret that I must inform you of the death of Private Andrew Parry, who was killed in action at…' I looked at Annie and saw tears dancing delicately down her cheeks.

'My Andrew was the sweetest boy you could ever meet. I know all mams think that about their boys, but mine was. The day he was conscripted was the worst day of my life, but he knew how to keep his old mam happy. He'd write me letters; about the sights he'd seen and the pals he'd made and the things he was looking forward to doing once he got home. Then, one day, the letters stopped.'

My stomach twisted and churned as Mrs. Parry spoke. 'What happened? If you don't mind me asking?' I said.

'He stepped on a land mine. I spent so long being angry about it, so long shutting out the memories of him so that I wouldn't have to feel the pain. And then I realised that he was still alive. Or that he could be. It was just down to me to make him so.' I must have looked confused because Annie smiled gently and said, 'What a batty old woman I must sound like. You see, on his birthday, I make him his favourite cawl and I bake him bara brith and I take out his letters and I read them over and over and I talk to him as if he was sitting right here beside me.'

'And that keeps him alive?'

'It does. For me. I think it could do the same for your mam,' said Annie.

'Her favourite food is shepherd's pie and I don't know how to make that,' I said.

Annie laughed, a deep, throaty laugh that resonated around the tiny kitchen.

'Come back and see me again and I'm sure I could show you.'

I left shortly after, my rucksack weighed down with breezeblock sized slices of bara brith wrapped in tinfoil and my flask refilled. I'm ashamed to say that I never returned to that little house in Cwmgwrach, despite the offer of culinary aid. It felt impertinent, like I was imposing myself on

8

something very private, and as my teenage years crept in, sullen awkwardness became my default. The thought of sharing my grief with Mrs. Parry became anathema. I thought about her often though, and every year, I make a batch of cawl and a loaf of bara brith for Private Parry's birthday. I hope it's half as good as his mother's.

*

It is now November 29th and I'm living on borrowed time. Like my mother was. Like Private Parry was, although he didn't know it then. I've thought long and hard about what I'd like to leave behind for you. You can have my records, of course, and your grandmother's best china. But I wanted to give you something special, something that would survive beyond me and even beyond you. This is it. A story. My story. I hope you take it out and read it when the nights are cold and you feel like I'm far away. I hope you read it so often that it becomes entwined in you, a little piece of me that no one can ever extract. Take care, my girl, be kind even when the world is not, and always remember that I love the bones of you.

P.S. If you should ever need a recipe for shepherd's pie, there's one pinned to the fridge.

Nathan Munday

23rd of October

On the twenty-third of October, Essex police discovered thirty-eight adults and one teenager who had passed away in a Bulgarian truck.

On the twenty-third of October,
the orange leaves and breeze
were disturbed by a sobering fact:
That thirty-nine sleepers were found in
a truck.

I didn't see their extinguished eyes
or distinguished their
figures in that fishy stomach – Jonahs
lapped by blackened space, and crates
creating misery
in that truck.

The doors were shut on autumnal light.
No blowhole or crack
for whispers of white to stripe the darkened
hope in that cold cave
of a truck

rocking like a boat through life.
Animals in their pens – two-by-two – squashed like cattle in
the flood's reversal. No longer was
the ark the bark of safety,
but a vessel of death in the form of a
truck.

No Noah there, just another bear
in a long line of growling drivers.
Essex and Auschwitz – blood-stained lands
where big dogs bark in Westminsters.
There is no policy candle which can switch
their eyes back on
the truck.

On the twenty-third of October,
the brown leaves and breeze
were silenced by a sobering fact:
That thirty-nine bodies were dead in
that truck.

Second Prize

Cara Cullen

Preiddeu Annwn

I look down to inspect the five little objects in my hand. Like cast-iron seed pods, they have hues of orange and blue and red drifting on their surface. They clink softly as I roll them around, nestled in my palm like beetles.

'Shells,' she says, 'ninety to one hundred million years old.'

I am sat on a train that winds slowly through green, torrential rain. The woman opposite me is tiny and white-haired with an enormous grin on her face; she looks straight at me.

'Shells,' she says again.

I'm feeling a bit flummoxed. I've just been out for a run on a rain-soaked mountain and I am covered in mud. I only just caught the train in time, jumping on as the doors shut. I can feel the water leaking out of my clothes and trainers into a puddle on the floor.

'You said you'd been running up on the tips!' she says laughing. 'That's where I find these fossils.'

'Oh right!' I say, still feeling a bit confused and holding out my hand as she continues watching me.

'Yeah,' she says. 'I was always out on the coal tips when I was young. My knees are too bad now.'

'So these were just lying around up there?' I ask. She can hear the sceptical tone in my voice.

'You take a look next time you go,' she says. 'A geologist showed me how to look for them when I was a teenager. He was a strange man he was; blue eyes like nothing you've ever seen. Clever mind you, and he knew all about fossils. Like the ones they've found on the top of Everest you know, they pop up out of the ground!'

I look back down at the shells and I remember my Grandad, stone-picking through the fields. He used to say that stones grew in the soil. Looking down at the little hinges and lips on these tiny fossilised clams makes me smile. Maybe he was right.

'You can keep those ones,' she says. 'I've got loads.'

'Are you sure?' I say, surprised.

'Yeah, you keep them,' she says, smiling.

She carries on watching as I put the stones down on the table where they rattle gently, dancing on the speckled plastic.

'It was a bad omen if you saw a fossil below ground of course,' she says suddenly.

I look back up to her and notice that her eyes are pale blue, watery around the edges. Her face is wrinkled and papery and there are crow's feet spreading out from her cheeks where the skin stretches around her grin.

'Miners used to think you would die if you saw a fossil underground. It meant you were going to have an accident; be squashed down flat!' She finishes the sentence with a little laugh.

'Really?' I say, slightly startled. 'I've never heard that before.'

I started to wonder if this woman was okay. She seemed friendly enough but she had been talking to me quite intensely since I sat down. There was something in her voice

13

and her openness that was a bit unnerving. She had three fat, breathless little dogs waddling under the table. I could see their heads move in and out of the shadow around her feet like a seething pile of wrinkled flesh.

Their tongues lolled out and they blinked slowly; their eyes bulging black. There was a strong wet-dog smell coming from them and I was trying not to breathe too deeply as I talked to her.

'That's a load of old rubbish, that is!' A voice bellowed out suddenly from the seat behind mine. A barrel-chested man wearing a dai-cap and thick glasses had leaned out from around the side of my seat and was staring belligerently at the woman.

'I've never heard that before and I worked underground!' he boomed.

The projection on his voice was impressive; it filled the carriage although I don't think he was trying to raise his voice. He sounded like a lifelong smoker; like his breath was clogged and narrow before it got to his lips.

'I've never heard about it anyway,' he said.

'Maybe it was before your time,' replied the woman, still smiling. Her finger had started tracing the outline of a tree in the mist on the window, she wasn't looking at him.

'Before my time! How old are you then love?' He spluttered indignantly and turned to look at me instead.

'We used to see loads of fossils underground,' he said. 'There were millions of them; leaves, insects, squirrels, rabbits. It was soft coal ours was, good for steam and the fossils would disappear as soon as you touched them. I've never heard of miners thinking they were going to die if they saw one.'

'I doubt you saw any rabbits in coal from the carboniferous period,' said the woman. She turned to look at him, her smile suddenly looked quite smug.

14

'Well, we'll bloody agree to disagree, is it?' he said, starting to look red around his neck. 'I saw rabbits and you can go around telling people that miners saw bloody death omens! What do you know about it anyway?'

He turned to me.

'Don't listen to her love, she's not all there, I reckon.' He tapped his forehead and nodded to the woman who was drawing on the window pane again.

'So you were a miner were you?' I asked him.

'Yeah, forty years down the pit, I was.'

He was staring at my face but through the thick glass, it didn't seem as though he could actually see me. He looked almost cross-eyed. He pulled himself closer; his hands gripping the polyester fabric. His fingers were thick and rigid, covered in broken veins from manual work and blood pressure tablets.

'There was one thing the old boys did believe though. I'd forgotten about it until now.'

He leaned in closer.

'When I was young, and I'm eighty now mind you; some of them would refuse to wash their backs. They said you would lose your strength if you washed the coal off your back. We never used to pay them any attention. I remember one of them, he had to go and get his lungs checked. We all had to go for these regular checks, like.

'Well, this one old guy, he was called back from the doctors and they told him they'd found a shadow on his lungs. You can imagine he was a bit worried and so back he went, expecting to hear the worst. It turned out it was all the coal dust on his back. They could see it in the X-ray, it was that thick!'

The man started to roar with laughter, his head thrown back for a full minute. He looked back at me. 'Hadn't had a bath in years!'

He retreated behind the seat out of view. I caught a glimpse of a woman who looked like his wife put her hand gently on his knee.

'What? I wasn't saying anything wrong. Kids don't know they're born today.'

I heard him mutter. Further up the aisle, I saw a priest listening as the miner spoke but he turned away to stare at his phone when he saw me smiling at him. His dog collar winked white from his all-black ensemble. He had a leather briefcase that looked expensive and I noticed that his raincoat was branded with the word "Trespass". I wondered if he had chosen it on purpose.

Almost everyone on the train seemed to be on their phones. There were two girls sat at another table, rhythmically swiping their fingers with little flicks on the rectangles of plastic in their hands. They looked so bored and so beautiful. Their faces were glistening bronze, and their eyebrows were stencilled into perfect arches over thick, black eyelashes like moths. The layers of paint made their skin look heavy over the spots and craters of teenage acne.

'What are you doing?'

An elderly woman dressed head-to-toe in pink and clutching a handbag was talking to her son. He looked like her son at least; long greasy hair slicked down with a comb. He wore a black jacket that was too big for him and the back of it was covered in flakes of dandruff. He slouched as if trying to make himself smaller.

'Just checking my accounts,' he answered.

Over the side of his arm, I caught a glimpse of the Instagram feed he was scrolling through. He paused on an image of a girl with long, black hair. She wore stockings and suspenders and a pink corset over a maid uniform. He scrolled past her.

'Oh excuse me.' An old man brushed past my arm. I watched as he walked slowly down the aisle, three-legged, with a knobbly wooden stick hitting the floor hard. He looked like he was in pain. He paused by the toilet door where the train bent and swung in the join between carriages. He slowly opened it and walked in. I caught a whiff of chemicals and sick. I suddenly realised as I looked around that there weren't many empty seats on the train. I hope he didn't go in there just to sit down.

'That's pretty.' The woman with the dogs had started talking to me again.

'Sorry, what's that?' I asked.

'That necklace you're wearing, it's very pretty,' she said.

I looked down at my T-shirt and picked up the gold coin that hung on the chain around my neck.

'Oh yeah, my Grandad gave me that. It's an old Irish coin with a peacock on it,' I said. 'He was Irish.'

I felt uncomfortable again about the woman who was staring at my chest with her fixed grin. The smell around her seemed to be getting stronger.

'That's the peacock from the Book of Kells then, isn't it?' she asked.

'I'm not really sure,' I said.

'Oh yes, I'm sure it is. In medieval times they used to believe that peacock flesh didn't rot, so it must be close to God. Like Buddhist monks, you know. They think the same thing. If you don't rot, you must be holy!' She laughed again.

I held my necklace in my hand and tried to avoid her gaze. I looked at what she had drawn on the window instead. There was a tree and a boat on top of lots of wavy lines, like a river.

'What have you drawn there?' I asked, trying to move the conversation away from me.

'Oh, just an old river,' she said, smiling. 'I forget its name.'

17

There was a sudden glow of sunlight from outside slanting sideways into the carriage and making the grey mist on the windows glow opaquely. The silhouette of her drawing was illuminated behind her and the bright green of the trees and sidings flashed past in the wonky lines like a stained glass window, inside-out.

Further down the carriage, the sun caught the eyes of the conductor who was finally walking towards me. For a moment she seemed to have white balls blazing inside their sockets. The rest of her face was in sunken shadow.

'You're a bit wet aren't you?' She laughed when she got to me.

'Yeah,' I said. 'I've been out running.'

'You should bring a towel with you next time,' she laughed. 'Where are you going then, love?'

I told her where I was getting off, watching as she tapped it into the ticket machine around her neck.

'That's £3.70 then, lovely.'

I started to root around for my card. It had been too hot to wear my coat while I was running despite the rain and it was tied in a messy, wet knot around my waist. I felt for the small pocket in the coat where I had put everything I had to keep safe. It was unzipped and empty.

'Oh my God, I'm so sorry. I think I've lost my bank card,' I said.

I couldn't quite bring myself to look her in the eyes, staring vaguely instead at the name badge on her jumper that told me "Your conductor's name is Sharon" while I patted my leggings and coat in a pretty futile attempt at a search. I knew that my card must be somewhere in amongst the Winberry bushes and the heather on top of the mountain. My heart started to race. I was kicking myself for getting on the train without checking I could pay first. I was almost home by now.

'That's a lovely thing you've got around your neck, isn't it?' said the conductor.

I looked down at my necklace again and back up at her. She was smiling.

Gareth Smith

Mam

Caroline's eyes traversed the nursing home. It had something of a holiday camp atmosphere. A false sense of optimism crackled like static electricity around the marshmallow pink building and its garden, neatly contained within a gate painted eggshell blue. A faded gnome faced her from the other side, watching with blind eyes.

Her next interviewee was somewhere in that geriatric Butlins and she couldn't have been less enthused. It was yet another 100th birthday. Her fourth of the year – and it was still only August.

There was no denying that centenarians were far less remarkable than they used to be. The numbers were increasing, but so were the certainties that the birthday boy or girl would be almost completely senile. Caroline would crouch in front of them with her notepad, spoon-feeding them inane questions that they rarely answered.

Do you remember the Second World War? Did you watch the Coronation?

Do you remember when they were called Opal Fruits?

Then, the worst part. Caroline would photograph their sagging and bewildered faces and, in the process, feel like she was subjecting them to a cruel practical joke. They were usually surrounded by a cross-generational circle of smiling family, either oblivious to their relative's complete lack of awareness or happy to ignore it.

Caroline pressed the electronic buzzer and the entire gate vibrated. She pushed it open and moved towards the front door. A care assistant, wearing a navy tabard and pink gloves, held it open with his knee.

'I can't stop. We're having a bit of an issue in the downstairs toilets.'

Caroline nodded, pretending not to notice the smell that immediately enveloped her as she entered the hallway. The care assistant marched away. Caroline called after him.

'I'm looking for Room 22.'

'Up the stairs, third right,' came the hurried response. 'And the code is 2-3-4-5.'

Caroline ascended the nearest set of stairs. Photographs of residents lined the wall, celebrating birthdays and holidays together. The initial smell lingered everywhere, pausing with Caroline between doors as she tapped the code before moving on to the next section of the building.

She walked down a long corridor with most of the doors closed. A wizened woman with short hair and sharp, alert eyes was pacing back and forth. Caroline wondered whether it would be patronizing or not to smile at her.

'Are you from the *Post*?'

She almost shrieked. There had been such little activity in the building, and most of it muted or mumbled, that the sudden appearance of a man in the doorway had been far more dramatic than it should have been. He was tall and stocky, probably in his fifties, with large features and a red, perspiring face. Although balding on top, he retained a thick halo of hair around and above his ears

'I'm Clive,' he said. His hand was as warm and sweaty as

she imagined his face to be. She turned to wipe it on her coat as he turned around. 'You've come to see Mam.'

The carpet was thick and bile green, something Caroline couldn't help but notice as her shoes became enveloped in its fluffy tangles. The wallpaper was peach and peeling a little in the corners.

The "Happy Birthday" balloons, cards, and gifts that were scattered about the place looked as though they were in storage for another, more cheerful, location. Several bouquets of flowers lined the windowsill next to the bed, blocking most of the light.

'We're very excited that she's going to be in the *Post*…' Clive continued enthusiastically. 'Mam used to get it every day before she moved here.'

Caroline bit her tongue to avoid muttering anything sarcastic. No-one was reading the *Post* anymore, herself included. It had never been the most exciting job in the world, but it always came with the adage: "it pays the bills". With circulation dwindling, "bills" was now barely singular.

As Clive's inane small talk continued, Caroline stepped tentatively closer to the figure that she had come to visit. She was, as usual, trying to assess whether the birthday girl would be even remotely self-aware. So far, it didn't look promising.

The bed was as clean and smooth and white as paper. The shape on it seemed barely to have disturbed it with her presence. She faced away. Her hair matched the bed in its colour, its thick tufts combed back against the pillow. Hands, darkened with veins, were knit together.

'Mam, you've got a visitor.'

The head turned. She was small – they were always small – with a sharp, angular face. She looked nothing like her son, whose features were rounded and fleshy. Her eyes, bloodshot and milky-blue, dipped lazily from Clive to Caroline.

'She's come to talk to you about your birthday, remember? You're going to be in the *Post*? Do you remember?'

He looked at Caroline with a humouring smile, one that she was very familiar with. She turned back to "Mam", having completely forgotten the woman's actual name. It was in an e-mail somewhere on her phone and it would look too obvious to check.

'It's nothing to worry about!' she said, hating herself for using the "I'm talking to an old person" voice that always struck her as that of a children's television presenter.

'Just a few questions and a photo so that we can let everyone know about your celebration. Won't take long.'

'What do you think, Mam?' His tone was similar, coaxing and indulgent.

She looked at Clive for a few seconds, aware he had spoken but seemingly clueless as to the meaning of his words. He seemed content to enjoy the silence, but Caroline had a golden wedding anniversary and a rescued dachshund to get to.

'I can just ask your son the questions if you'd prefer?'

Clive's smile widened, exposing some of the lunch he'd had earlier in the day. He raised his hands lightly in protest.

'I'm her grandson. My mother passed away a few years ago.'

'Oh, I'm sorry – '

'It's fine. It's fine.' He sat down on one of the chairs and invited Caroline to do the same.

'Everyone calls her Mam, you see, whether they're related or not. She's what you'd call a typical Welsh Mam. Do you know what I mean?'

Caroline nodded.

'Everyone in the village knows her. She's a bit of a celebrity up there.'

She turned to Mam for a flicker of a smile. Nothing.

23

Clive continued, 'She's had eight children. Eight! You can't imagine it today, can you? All in a council house that wasn't fit for purpose. She had the first when she was twenty-one and the last when she was thirty-eight. I think they were made of sterner stuff in those days.'

'It's a big family then?' Caroline asked.

'It used to be. But a few of the kids moved away. She's outlived some of them too, which was difficult – wasn't it, Mam? But there are a lot of grandchildren and great-grandchildren and such like.'

'I bet she enjoys seeing them.'

Caroline could tell that Mam was listening to the conversation. She was pretending not to but there was a look of concentration on her face, and sometimes her lips moved as though she were trying to mime what Clive was saying.

'They come when they can. I'm the main one here now. It's easier I suppose, because I'm divorced and I work nights... but I think she'd love to see more of the little ones, wouldn't you, Mam?'

Caroline and Clive chatted for the next few minutes, outlining the details of Mam's life as if preparing her eulogy. She had been a member of the ladies' choir, had shaken Nye Bevan's hand and had protested the closure of the local primary school. She baked wonderful bara brith and had stopped attending Bingo only two short years ago. She loved *Strictly Come Dancing* and *Pointless* and had once appeared in the audience of *The Generation Game*.

Caroline had stopped writing by the end, already knowing she had more than enough for the article.

'How about a photo?' she asked abruptly, cutting across Clive's reminisces of a typical Christmas at Mam's.

'You don't mind having your picture taken, do you Mam?'

he said, looking her squarely in the eyes. 'I told you there'd be one. That's why we've got you looking so nice.'

There was an awkward silence which Caroline tried to fill by rummaging through her bag for the camera. When she finally pulled it out, opened the lens and looked up, they were still staring at one another.

'One photo, Mam. One photo, that's all.'

She made a brief, barely audible sound, something guttural at the back of her throat.

'Iawn.' Her voice was firm but weakened, even the one word conveying a sense of struggle. Clive moved around the bed. He helped Mam adjust the pillows behind her back so that she was sitting up straight. He put his arm around her and gave a big, toothy smile.

Caroline hid her amusement; it had seemingly never occurred to him that he wouldn't be in the photo. Mam's mouth curled at the edges like stale sandwiches, but there was no warmth in her expression.

'Say cheese!' Clive shouted as the flash went off.

Caroline squinted to check the quality of the photo on-screen and faintly noticed an object rushing towards her head. She reacted in time to throw herself back and witness a small plastic vase flying through the air, shedding stalks as it ascended. It hit the wall behind her with a musical clang and bounced off the door. Water ran in pale streaks against the wallpaper.

'Mam!' Clive barked the word.

He looked immediately at Caroline in apology. She turned to stare at the vase, now rolling on its side in the corridor, and was amazed that such a delicate old lady had mustered the strength to throw it in the first place. There was a noticeable gap on the windowsill next to her.

'It's okay...' Caroline said as Clive bustled past her to pick it up.

'I don't know what's gotten into her.'

Clive left the room. As soon as he did, Mam's eyes flared. She turned to Caroline, animated with purpose.

'I'm not his Mam!' her voice croaked. 'I don't know who he is.'

Caroline almost jerked forward in surprise. She opened her mouth to speak but Mam hurried on, desperate to get her words out.

'He can't be. I never had children. He just turned up here one day. He tells the stories…he tells me they're real…they're not. I'm not his Mam! I'm not…'

Caroline felt a gasp of warm air on the back of her neck and flinched. Clive was behind her, holding the sopping vase and discarded flowers in each hand. He sighed and shook his head.

'It's awful to hear her say things like that,' he said solemnly. 'But you get used to it. I hope she hasn't upset you.'

Mam stared pleadingly at Caroline. Clive walked further into the room.

'You've just got to try your best to keep reminding them,' he said. 'Ask anyone here. It's heart-breaking. But you do it out of love…'

Caroline chose to ignore this and asked Mam directly: 'Can you say that again?'

Mam's head was back on the pillow.

Clive tried talking again but Caroline cut him off to repeat her question. Mam looked ahead. The brittle fingers curled over one another as she placed her hands over the blanket. It was like watching a mechanical toy wind down to its original position after a brief spasm of activity.

Clive apologised vehemently. He said that her dementia had been getting progressively worse and that such outbursts were becoming increasingly bizarre. As normality descended on the room again, Caroline found herself feeling stupid for even having considered any other possibility. A few minutes later, and following another moist handshake, she found herself descending the stairs again. She did hover briefly in the foyer, hoping to ask a member of staff a little more about Mam. Perhaps, if she was lucky, find out whether Clive was listed as her next of kin.

Nobody came. She trudged back to her car. Clive waved from the window.

Editing the article later that evening, Caroline couldn't help returning to the photograph. The sickly colours of the room provided a frame for the central tableau of the painfully white bed and the two figures upon it. Mam's frail body seemed enveloped by Clive; his meaty forearm was coiled around her neck. The bold hue of his face reduced hers to near translucence. However, despite the insistence that she fade into the background of her own birthday photograph, something defiant remained.

Caroline found a thought unfurling in her mind before she could stop it. Imagine if she's telling the truth. Then, immediate denial. It was too ridiculous. Outlandish. Impossible. Clive had seemed vaguely irritating, but not insane.

But what if she's telling the truth?

What if overworked staff haven't noticed what's going on?

What if he's just turning up there once a week?

What if…but then, the bigger question. Why?

That was where the argument fell apart. Caroline found herself typing out the headline: *Nursing-Home Hoax: Man Forces Stranger to Be His 'Mam'*. It worked surprisingly well with the photograph and added an eeriness to the image. For a moment, and it was a very fleeting moment, she considered sticking with it.

With very pointed taps on the keyboard, Caroline erased her words. There were headlines that fit and headlines that didn't. The new one barely took a second to write.

100 Years Young: 'She's Mam to Everyone' Says Proud Grandson

Elizabeth Rose Choi

The Middle Room

Nobody tells you when you've done enough. There are no guidelines for how far you should intervene in the lives of others. Yet the window for making a genuine difference in their life, you'd be surprised to find, is smaller than a slither. And when you miss that window, you are left feeling blind, or heartless, or even in some cases, cruel. At least, that is what I have felt.

Arianwen and I often saw Mrs Griffiths in the park. She lived in one of the neat Georgian houses overlooking it. She played bridge with my mother, so we knew her, in a second-hand sort of way. Whenever her dogs bounded into the park, all eyes were on them. Two of the most gorgeous greyhounds you ever saw and they knew it. They adored our attention, rubbing their sides up against our knees. Yet there was one thing they loved more than both of these things, and that was their mistress. It was rare that they were ever more than ten feet away from her for any length of time. We were watching them from the benches, that day, doing their laps as usual. That was when we heard the shout.

'Just leave it. Can't you tell you've done enough!' The words echoed across the park. I was sure it was loud enough for everyone to hear, but if they did they never batted an eyelid. Yet Ari's eyes were wide. She'd noticed all of it and more. Something neither I nor anyone else in the park had heard. A deep, unsubdued sob from across the park.

'Keren, can you see over behind the tennis courts?' Ari whispered, fidgeting with the end of her nose. I craned my neck to see the place she'd nodded towards, just in time to see a young mother storming down the path, half dragging her toddler along with her. She had left an old woman crumpled in the hedge. The two greyhounds faithfully back by her side.

Ari leapt up, and I followed close behind her. Mrs Griffiths remained crouched, covering her face with one hand, bracing herself against the swaying bush with the other. A bag of toys and dolls had been strewn across the path. I left Ari to comfort the woman, and I set out to refill Mrs Griffiths' IKEA bag with the misplaced toys.

'Hey, it's okay, it's okay.' Ari crouched beside her, hesitantly smoothing her shoulder. Mrs Griffiths flinched, but then looked up with the kindest eyes. They were red at the rim, and her cheeks were all flushed and blotchy.

'I'm sorry, it is terribly embarrassing.' She took in a sharp breath, and then exhaled slowly, shutting her eyes briefly and raising her head to the sky. 'I'm fine, really. I'll only be a moment... so embarrassing... was just a misunderstanding, honestly.' She kept nodding as she rolled forward onto her knees, and then took Ari's arm with a tremoring hand to get the rest of the way up. Even at her full height, she was small, and her clothes hung loosely from her frame. She wore a pair of green corduroys and a sleeveless cardigan over her blouse: the sort all pensioners love, but you never seem to see in the shops.

'Can we get you anything? A drink, maybe?' As Ari spoke Mrs Griffiths turned to look up at her, softened by this unexpected kindness. I thought she was about to accept, but then she shrank away again, shaking her head, her thin bob quivering with each movement.

'I don't live too far away, wouldn't want to waste your money.' She sighed slowly and carefully lifted her chin high.

'Well, if you don't live far then will you let us walk you back?' At this the woman paused, considering. She gazed out at something over the hedges, the row of houses above the park; but then she dismissed whatever she had been thinking, nodding back at us with a toothy grin.

We hobbled with her around to the park entrance, and up to her house. The dogs weren't far behind. They slid their way inside the house when the smallest slither of a gap opened. They bounded straight to the back of the house, leaving the three of us in the hallway. It was narrow, with tall ceilings, and the dated lampshade cast a dull orange light, leaving much of the house still obscured in the dim. Mrs Griffiths took off her shoes, setting them in place between her wellingtons and sandals. The wallpaper behind them had warped, like skin on a snake about to shed. An old Viennese clock hung squarely in the middle of this wall, along with a pair of paintings; the kind you'd get for 50p in a charity shop.

'Shall I pop this anywhere? Or?' I tentatively held up the bag of toys. Mrs Griffiths hummed, taking it from me and placing it in the middle room, shutting the door almost as quickly as she had opened it. From the glimpse I stole, the room wasn't a large one, but the natural light seemed to seep out of the cracks in the door.

'Tea?' Mrs Griffiths leant forwards and said lightly, as though she were treating us to luxury. We were led down some steps into the kitchen, where the dogs had already made a beeline for their bowls. Since the terrace had been built into a hill, all you could see from the kitchen window was the steep slate steps, which gave the room an icy air. We shuffled onto a converted pew tucked behind the table. My mind danced with the brief explanation our hostess had given us on the walk across. The young mother, disgusted that Mrs Griffiths had been handing out toys to her child, had let her temper get the better of her. I supposed people didn't trust anyone these days. I thought of times in my own life where I thought I knew a person, only to find that they were capable of things far worse than I would ever have dreaded. I looked up to find Mrs Griffiths leaning against the countertop, looking dully at the tiled floor as she waited for the kettle. Ari, too, was preoccupied with her thoughts.

'She shouldn't have reacted like that, you know,' Ari muttered, thumbing her upper lip in reflection. Mrs Griffiths only sighed, and set down a teapot and a dish of pink wafers on the table. She had the softest green eyes that followed each movement her hands made.

'There's the park warden, or even the police I suppose?' I began, but a sharp breath from our host silenced me. It was only once she'd poured us all a cup of tea that she began to speak. She explained that it had happened before, albeit less dramatically than today.

'You must understand, dears, she's no stranger. She's my daughter, Livy.'

'I'm so sorry, I didn't mean to—' I flushed.

'No lovey, don't you worry. It was wrong of her, you're right. But I understand her—more than anybody ever will. No, she moved back in when she had little Emma, but, well, I don't know… it was different at home, with a little one. It was difficult for all of us, if you take my meaning.' Mrs Griffiths fidgeted with the button on her cardigan. After a moment she rubbed her face, let her hands trail down to the back of her neck, and spluttered, 'Anyway, she moved out around a year ago.'

'Yes, I know, it's hard,' Arianwen said quietly, almost to herself.

'Hard doesn't even begin to cover it,' she said, slightly more harshly than we had expected, 'she didn't choose to leave. She didn't decide it would somehow make her life easier, why would it ever be that black and white?' Mrs Griffiths bent over, urging us to do the same. We were so close that I could smell the stale coffee lingering on her breath. 'Why would she *decide* to leave a home where she wanted for nothing? She didn't ever have to worry about food or bills. Why would she leave? I gave her everything. Everything.' She looked deep into our eyes, scanning for any trace of understanding. Mrs Griffiths threw a sudden glance to the ceiling, before lowering her head back over her tea and leaving us in silence once again.

'I'm sorry.' I sighed, looking down into the dregs of my drink. I still had so many questions. I couldn't see why there would be such distance between them, why a daughter would leave her mother clinging to a bush, without even looking back.

Mrs Griffiths rose from the table, and began collecting the china.

'No, I'm sorry — don't you worry, pet. You've already done so much to help me…I do appreciate it so, thank you.' She didn't even look over her shoulder as she said this, but kept her head down as she swilled out the teapot.

'I… uh… I don't want this to come off the wrong way, Mrs Griffiths, but well, I don't live very far away,' Arianwen began, fiddling with the lace tablecloth, 'what I'm trying to say is that, well, if you're ever in need. If you're ever in any trouble — even just like today — would you like my phone number? Even just to talk, if you want.'

At this, Mrs Griffiths seemed to freeze, until she turned slowly and looked Arianwen directly in the eyes, with the same intensity as before. After a moment her features softened, but she remained fixed still, doing her best to read the woman before her.

'Oh sweetie.' She relaxed, and clasped her hands together as she spoke. 'I'll just go get it… my phone, I keep it upstairs. Wouldn't want to break it or lose it if I took it out of the house.' She shuffled down the hallway and we started to follow, but she told us there was no need us all going and so left us at the foot of the stairs.

I suppose it was inevitable that we ended up in the middle room. The fresh light came in through a pair of tall French windows, revealing the dust particles we'd been breathing in this whole time. The walls were clad in the same aged wallpaper as the rest of the house, but in here they still held the pulse of a living, loved room. Shelves filled with curious teddies and dolls lined the walls; in fact, every surface of this room was filled with some sort of toy or trinket.

I had been distracted by the ornaments and hadn't noticed Ari join me in the room. She had been drawn to a small butterfly box at the foot of the armchair, which she was now sat in, bent over a heap of papers on her lap.

'Ari?'

Her head snapped up when I spoke, her eyes red around the rim.

'I know it, Ker, I'm not reading too much into this… something is wrong.' Her voice cracked as the words tumbled out.

'What?' I crouched next to her and tried to take the papers from her hands, but she only grasped them tighter.

'You have to look, properly. See?' She fanned the drawings out. Children's drawings.

'Pictures? Just kid's pictures.'

Ari stiffened at my bluntness; her brows drawn. 'How old was that kid in the park, would you say? One? Two at a push? Sure, the drawings are in crayon, but look—' She handed them over to me. Arianwen was right. The majority of them, although scruffy, were far too complex for a child of that age. Each of them were sketches, the mother's sketches, of this room: the Russian doll on the mantelpiece, the details in the old wooden door, all items I could see from where I sat crouched.

'So, she drew what was around her? I don't get it?'

'That's not it. Look, closer.' I was about to tell her she'd gone overboard when I spotted it. I had missed it at first glance, but there was a shadow to these drawings. There was a dark figure hidden in the mirror above the mantelpiece, blackness seeping from the ceiling dripping like tar, and perhaps the most hauntingly, the eye in the keyhole of the door. I glanced up at Ari, but as I did there was an almighty thud from upstairs that made the lampshade rattle. My breath caught in my throat.

'It's so wrong, Ker,' Ari whimpered. A figure shifted in the corner of my eye. I jolted to my feet. It was Mrs Griffiths, pale and breathless in the doorway.

'He can't know you're here... he can't.' Her voice was steadier than before. 'So, either in or out.'

She held a key in one hand and reached for the handle of the door. She quivered, but held her head high, repeating herself in the same rasp tone. I still had so many questions, but they no longer mattered. I grabbed for Arianwen's hand and made a dash for the door. Mrs Griffiths stepped out of the way, still shaking and casting fearful glances to the stairs above her. Heavy footsteps echoed down the landing. The dogs fled for the door but halted in line with their mistress, who held the front door open, ready for our escape. He'd made it partway down the stairs as she shut the door, and we saw no more. All we heard through the solid oak was the shrill whines of the greyhounds.

Emily Hancox

Aberdulais Bwbach

Bwbach is a creature that most won't know
They scuttle in shadows
they keep their heads low.
They come in many sizes,
they creep through locks
and shimmy through doors
they mend all things broken
and finish undone chores.

Allow me to show you,
let me spread a little light
on our very own Bwbach
that we caught earlier tonight.
He's nimble and bony
he's full of Welsh sass
He's been living under our waterwheel
he's an Aberdulais bwbach.

We lay nets on site,
we kept a keen eye
to see if we could capture and trick
our little guy.
He skipped out of our traps
he teased all our staff

but when he knew you were coming
he couldn't keep away
and he came straight back.

He loves to watch from a distance,
then creep a little near
he may look a little odd,
but never fear.
He's a friendly Bwbach
that loves to play tricks
if anything goes missing
he'll find it
pretty quick.
When our waterwheel can't turn
he's somewhere near by,
with his tool box in hand
he's brain scratching and hatching a plan!

He slips into the turbine,
and twists the loose screw
with some magic and muscle
the jobs done, and water sprouts through.
The waterwheel powers up
and the wheel starts to spin
and with no one else to see him
he dances a happy jig.
You see,
Bwbachs love a challenge,
they love a tricky job,
but more than anything, they love doing something
humans can't solve.

He's a shy little Bwbach,
but he does like to say *Hi*,
and if you see him on your visit,
wave, call out, or just smile.
He'll appreciate your gesture
and remember your kindness
and maybe if you have something broken
our little bwbach
might just fix it.

Cara Cullen

Fossils

Lying in bed, safe tucked and warm,
Cool light washes the star-strewn night,
The harvest moon is up and clear,
Waxing gold on the cresting dusk,
Now garbed in cruel white.

Beneath the bones of the mountain,
Across the valleys and the hills,
In day, undressed of all their charm,
The sterile past is masked and smooth
And walks the lighted land.

Glimpsed only in the turning lanes,
The valley sides too deep to dress,
The unbounded stream, wandering,
Stone things hidden among the rest
And the lost eyes, soulless.

Under death cold fingers, guiding,
Father time steps idly backward,
And the ghosts come gaily strolling
From the hills all wreathed white and black,
The fossils, hand in hand.

Where once, men and Morfydd women
Went unto the glisten, jet, seams,
To cut, to dress and to plunder,
The harvest gold, the harvest black,
Where slack, oil tears were drunk,

Now, come smiling ghosts, street thronging,
To dream their nightmare as before,
And in our dreams, as we shudder,
Beneath that golden diskèd sky,
Dread growing at our core,

The creeping fear, the glancing eye,
Returns sharp, bright and on its edge.
Do not disturb that omen dread,
The black dog lying in its bed,
Nor raise the grave hound head.

Hark! Words are whispered in the deep,
The white teeth in the dark of time.
Those bodies lying in their sheath
Mutter soft from the slag-tip depths,
'Ah, I have seen the leaf.'

And in glorious harmony,
The celebrant breath, the last call,
A gale-force chorus from the slump,
The great barrow hall of propped limbs,
'Oh, I have seen the fall.'

Children too, were stopped in their tracks,
With lesson-book heads, pressed down flat,
To join the didacts down below

And round mouths, eternal, singing,
'Help! Please! Excelsior!'

For down under our feet so deep,
Are bodies beloved, lying flat,
Who lie unstirring in their mould,
Preserved in time, for ages old,
Like fossil leaves, growing.

I heard of a boy
who took pictures

I heard of a boy who took pictures
Of gold
Because he liked the light burnished
Into his soul
And I said, 'keep your gold,
For I have the sun.'

A young man came to steal the sun
Who laughed,
Covered by a veil of smoke, spelling
'Do not look'
And I said, 'I love the light
Of those angry clouds.'

I read about the man grown up
Inside towers
Where golden smokers live,
Proud and gilt
With the riches of pictures
Only they can see

And I said, 'keep your pictures,
For I have the hawthorn tree
Bent in the field.'

Rhys Swainston

The Martyr

I don't need you to believe me. I just need you to hear me out.

There sits, some two streets away from my house in Swansea, an old apartment complex. All the curtains are drawn. The lights stay off. There are never cars parked on the driveway. Nobody tends to the beds of Indian pipe plants growing in the boxes on the first-floor balcony. The building just *exists*, an assemblage of empty rooms and dark, dusty corridors. I know all of this because I've been there. I have been to Martyr's Reach. And God help me, I will not go again.

The Reach was, a very long time ago, a set of amenity flats designed for the supported care of older people. Picture an old folks' home, only with separate accommodation for each resident. The glum little block sat at the end of St. Alban's Road in the Brynmill area, the same area that I live to this day. It's a dreary looking building, perhaps fitting given its status as a care home, though it certainly isn't worthy of its rather grandiose title. Its walls are an off-white colour, stained with brown and yellow from the years it has spent suffering on this earth. Its front door is old and faded red, an optimistic colour. Maybe an attempt to brighten up the place? If it were, it hadn't done any good. It is a ghastly sight of a building, born out of an architect's exhaustion. It's not even that tall, barely earning the name complex. It only reaches up three floors before the grey slanted roof cuts it off from the sky. Even old photographs I've found online show it to be a glum place. Its dreariness shines through the grainy black and white images like a hand reaching through the page to grab at you.

In summary, I rather liked it.

It was perfect for me. You see, old abandoned buildings were somewhat of a hobby of mine. Take a flashlight and a crowbar and go and investigate. Urban exploration, it's called. I never knew exactly what I hoped to find in these places, aside from the adrenaline rush I experienced from being somewhere I knew I shouldn't be. Perhaps that was all I went there for, that child-like need to be excited, to break the rules. And I could never resist Martyr's Reach, not an empty vestige so near my home.

I had previously visited several similarly destitute dwellings. My first was St Catherine's Fort on its namesake island off the coast of Tenby. A rather more interesting place than the Reach, it must be said. It was an old army base that sits empty now, save for the tourists that flock to it looking for something to do. My parents took me and my brother, and while they stood around cold and disinterested, I explored. The next was the Denbigh Hospital and Asylum, up in the north. I went expecting fear, the screams of long-dead patients, scratchings on the walls and a whole other assortment of hauntings dreamt up by my impulsive imagination. Instead, I found a set of broken grey buildings and more tourists. I needed to find a place to be alone.

A quick drive through Powys brought me to another asylum, this one smaller than Denbigh, and the famous Red Dress House, though I only got to look at it from a distance. And of course, my most recent jaunt until the Reach, the Palace Theatre in my hometown. Abandoned for years, it sits dilapidated in the centre of High Street, Swansea. I confess I broke in one night (a little drunk) and made my way to the stage inside. Every footstep, every breath echoed dryly through the enormous room, pitch black, save for the blue light of my torch. Standing on the stage, I bowed and basked in imaginary applause, as though the theatregoers from long ago were praising my break-in.

All these buildings have one thing in common; they are far more interesting than Martyr's Reach. Their stories stretch through time and they are filled with the ghosts of their pasts. So why do I sit here and write about the Reach? Because those other buildings may be filled to bursting with history, but I saw none of it. Nothing lives in the Palace Theatre, or the fort in Tenby, or any of the other places I visited. There scream no screams at Denbigh Asylum.

Are you still with me? I hope you are. I just need you to hear this out and then our business together is done. You can go back to your life, as I have tried to go back to mine. You, no doubt, will have better luck than me. And please. Don't tell me you have a worse one.

I chose a drizzly overcast Tuesday for my next adventure. I took no safety equipment, only my torch and the crowbar I'd taken from my father's toolbox many years ago. I hoped at the time to break open enough doors with it as to wear away the end to nothing. That is the mark of a tested explorer; how timeworn their tools are. Mine sits today in my cupboard, very much intact.

The first and most important rule of exploration is, of course, to let someone know where you're going. My closest friend Marnie was not impressed.

'You could have got arrested last time, you idiot,' she snapped at me over the phone as I left my house. 'You were lucky you weren't. Not skilful, or cool or anything like that. Just lucky!'

'You've got faith in me then,' I joked, but Marnie wasn't

wrong. It only took one neighbour peeking out of their window and seeing a figure pushing through a window in the complex and I would spend the rest of the day staring at the opposite wall of a police cell.

'That's why I go in the day, see?' I explained. 'Everyone's out. St Alban's is all nice houses; people with jobs own them. They're not in at noon, so I'll be fine.'

'Sure. Well, I can't stop you, can I?' Marnie's voice sounded bitter over the phone.

Her usual other attacks were, *'You'll get hurt!'* or, *'You'll fall through the floor!'*. However, both of these scenarios were unlikely, given that the Reach had only been abandoned ten years ago due to not being able to keep up with the costs.

'No, you can't,' was all I said and hung up. I didn't like her tone. A little too condescending for my liking. She'd never liked me exploring, ever since I told her about my performance at the Palace Theatre. I would never have admitted that she was right because admitting it might have stopped me from going. And I thought I'd never stop.

The Reach stood where it had always stood, at the end of the road, jutting a pathetically short distance above the roofs of the neighbouring houses. Empty, or so I thought. With no sign of anyone around to witness my misdeeds, I circled to the back of the complex and vaulted over the small brick wall surrounding it. The back door was a metal fire door, too solid for me to prise open with my crowbar, so I crept back out to the front to find the main door. Thankfully, it was wooden and looked much older than the back door. I drew my crowbar from the inside of my jacket and, with a quick cautionary glance around for passers-by, jammed the end into the door frame. There came the then all-too-familiar crack of splintering wood and shavings of faded red paint rained down onto my boot as I pushed on the crowbar as hard as I could. Eventually, the door gave way with another loud crack and I stumbled forward, the crowbar clattering to my feet. Immediately, I was back on my feet, scanning the road for anyone who might have heard the din. Nothing.

I pushed my way inside the complex. Suddenly, in a wave of adrenaline, I became transfixed with the beauty of the dilapidated building. The foyer was empty save for an old desk, grey with dust and infested with woodworm. Behind it sat an equally dusty reclining chair that at some point in its life must have been comfortable, but which now sat alone and daunting, a ghost of its former self. I, of course, sat in it and gazed excitedly around as the pale noon sunlight slid through the open door. The walls were stripped of paint and plaster, with old wires and wood panels poking out at odd angles. The carpet here had been torn away; its edges still clinging on to the bottom of the grey skirting that ran around the room. None of this may seem beautiful to you, I know, but consider me. At this point in my life, I was bored, penniless and far removed from the things most people would call luxuries. There was no fancy house waiting for me when I left, no expensive holiday to some remote land, no big art galleries or museum exhibits nearby, the sorts of places filled with wonder and allurement. It couldn't even be said that the town was beautiful, despite its beaches and parks. It was always so grey.

No, the beauty of Martyr's Reach was in me, in how it made me feel, and since abandoning my favourite hobby I have never seen or felt beauty like it. The foyer housed such imagination, such symmetry. I could sit and wonder at all the people who came and went through that faded red door. I could explore the rooms and dream of the history of the place, through the various flats of the residents. I pictured an old woman sat in her now empty armchair writing a letter to a grandchild. I envisioned a gentleman looking at himself in the now broken mirror hanging from a bedroom wall, straightening his tie and smiling to himself. I visualised a man sitting at his —

A heavy thud sounded from upstairs.

The dead lightbulb above my head swung from the impact and a sharp breath rang through my chest. In all my time exploring old buildings, I had never heard anything, save for my footsteps echoing on the stone floors and the chattering of birds. I looked up. I hadn't yet reached the top floor.

I pulled the crowbar back out from my jacket pocket. It slid from my hand and hit the wooden floor with a clang so loud I almost cried out myself. From above, there immediately came a harsh scurrying sound, like a rat scrambling along the floor but bigger and heavier. Then came a strange shriek, like something scraping on glass, and more scurrying, then silence.

I could have left. I knew it, I could have turned and fled down the stairs to the faded red door and retreated to my house. But adrenaline is an addictive drug. Before I knew what I was doing, my feet were tiptoeing me out of the flat I was in as softly as they could. I could feel the cold steel of the crowbar back in my hand, though I had no memory of picking it up. And then, before I knew it, I was at the top of the stairs, and staring at an open window at the end of the landing. I had scouted the place before coming here. *The Reach had no open windows!*

I felt like going to poke my head out to see who, or what, had opened it. A squatter maybe? That seemed the most likely option. A homeless person, wandering in to keep the cold at bay, only to scurry away once he heard someone downstairs. I'd probably frightened the poor man half to death, especially since he felt that his best course of action had been to climb out of a third-storey window. I mean, how afraid must you be to —

Please read on. And please believe me. I was lying before. I do need you to believe. Because no man moved the way this creature moved.

I first saw only its head, a mess of tangled black hair covering its face. I could not see its eyes; I don't even know if it had eyes. Next came the hands, black with grime and dirt, long fingernails clawing at the windowpane as it dragged itself through the open window and slumped to the floor. Then, it stood, on all fours like a lizard, staring at… me? The floor? Nothing? All I did was stare in horror and revulsion, too frightened to even move as this creature from the depths of my worst nightmares began to sway side to side and snarl. Then it charged.

I turned and fled, the pounding of my boots on the floor barely masking the clacking of the thing's fingernails as it scurried after me. I tore down the stairs and slammed my way through the red door and didn't stop running until I was outside my front door. It took me three attempts to push the key into the lock and turn it and as soon as I was through I locked it behind me and collapsed in a heap on the floor, tears filling my eyes. My heart went mad.

I sat there motionless for maybe twenty minutes. Then I sent Marnie a text telling her I was fine and back home. I did not mention the creature. I received no reply from her. In the corner of my eye, a white petal fell from my shoulder onto the floor. It must have come from those pipe plants above the door. I brushed it away and shuddered. And then, as best as I could, I went about my day as though nothing out of the ordinary had happened.

I wonder sometimes, did the creature follow me to my house? Sometimes I dream of it, all these years later, scratching away at my front door and snarling. Sometimes I think, does it know where I live? Or, did it stay behind that red door, stay in its hovel, the ruin we call Martyr's Reach? Perhaps the stories about not being able to keep up payments were true but maybe there was more to them abandoning the place than it has always appeared. In any case, my most fearful jaunt was also my last; I may have left the Reach intact, but my passion had not. It's still there locked away with that awful creature. The one real pleasure I had in life was taken, and now, I feel as hollow and soulless as the buildings I used to love to frequent. Never again.

As for the creature, that final resident of Martyr's Reach, I hope it's happy. God help me if it should decide to take up the hobby I left there and go exploring.

Megan Charlton

Walking alone, draws winter in

The feeling of a warm hug,
like the freshness of sun-gloaming autumn leaves,
yearning for warmth before winter.

Naively wishing for a touch,
knowing everyone wants to feel that they are loved:
is preciously sharp, like the scent of earth after rain.
A tap on the shoulder given in solidarity, is spun into a
    fragile web to last a week.
The feeling of loneliness is half within your vision,
like a large mottled spider, hanging within a delicious
    blackberry bush.

The cool night air is swirling,
and there is a taste of winter on my tongue.

Kitchen ties capsize,
just as the waves up-writhe,
splashing a drenching spray strong,
in an almighty, unfurling wrong.

Winter is a sharp frost, burning nostrils,
in the cold like a lonely heart.

There is a keenness in my heart,
tarnished day and night, with a flurry of missed connections,
almost friends, held just out of reach by their flakiness,
evening and morning. I could waste wishing for friendship
held with equivalence and grace.

But winter is coming, chasing people indoors,
away into a dark solitude.
I wonder if you all, have a keenness,
a deep longing for kindness,
a fire in your blood,
an iced fear in your heart.
Or has the fire in your eyes being extinguished?
And you no longer seek love?

The fire can push into a burning fury of productivity,
Or boil into anger at past stupidity,
Or rise thrusting deep, like a dagger of grief.
A hot-cold heart, feverish with anxiety;
daily walks a ghost town.
The dagger morphs into a scalpel,
piecing self-motivation,
and scraping the self into hollowed pit,
of loneliness.

A soul wrapped up in nihilism,
slowly exudes a pitiful aura,
that buffets some away,
and causes others to pray upon naive eagerness.
Little wonder no fuck boy ever texts unequivocally,
nor holds any text-conversation equally,
they play the waiting game, drawing out your last ragged hopes,
to crush them all with one word replies to whole paragraphs.

I am walking through an autumn wood,
feeling wind-fettered,
pacing my life off,
with a pocket of hopeless expectations,
and the sense summer has ended.

Nathan Munday

Death of Tadcu Preacher

He lay in the clinic – an inventory of life.
Ticked-off parts
sewn together by thin,
layers of skin.

No brass or books or bara brith,
or clocks that chimed before the hour.
No Delius, Elgar, or Vaughan Williams.
Just monitors in the corner

Beeping.

Mamgu was like Magdalene,
and my mother's hair was damp with tears.
Tadcu had bruises on his hand and
his body was the final stand.

We wept with anger and prayed that
the stone could be rolled across
the day.

His hair waved across his head.
This wet ocean. This stinging salt.
This haunting depth was dark.

His eyes were fixed and free to roam
as if some spectre walked the foam.

He heard singing in the ward
And held my hand like a buoy.

A thin place.

His breath rattled like a cello
before the final note of vibrato.

And I lost him...

The slow pendulum of life
and those chimes from his pulpit
were laid in the ground
like an antique shroud.

Morgan Owen

Lightward

And the ghost fled lightward
     from its bones
scattered in a thistled hollow.

He'd long gathered dew
and drowned a thousand times
     in a haze
of flies: adrift,
shipwrecked among rotting plants;

he'd been born again
in a fall of maythorn flowers
     and every spring
that draws long grass
       and orchids
through a place
where his memory was.

Released by the moonlight,
silver on off-white;
he broke like seafoam
on a lunar landscape
of tips and craters
taken over by
     birch and oak.

Alexandra O'Leary

The Shrieking Decade

The infectious tune did little but encourage Fredrick of his chances with the beautiful blonde across the room. Ellington soothed his aching intellectual mind, encased in its very own curtain of wild brown hair. Of course, Fredrick knew the true cause of his motivation could be traced back to the poison that swirled around his glass and burned down his throat. Regardless, he watched her through velvet eyes as she swirled, twirled and stepped her way around the dance hall. Laughter and melodies carried her through the smoke towards him, causing a swift breath to rise into his chest as he caught a closer glimpse of her ocean eyes. Fredrick nodded to himself, leaning over to his friend confidently.

'I'm going to dance,' he informed him, hazily placing his glass down and beginning to rise. Scotty dismissed him as he put one foot before the other.

'I've never seen Fred there dance better than a newborn doe.'

Laughter roared behind the tall sanguine man as he approached the floor. Fredrick, prior to his overwhelming interest in a certain dancer, had been content simply tapping his foot off-beat (and occasionally on-beat.) But it couldn't be helped; he had to talk to the floating angel before he lost her forever. Awkwardly, in accordance to his awkward limbs, Fredrick jived over to his girl.

'Excuse me!'

Her eyes met his over the sound of the trumpets and suddenly the sparkling lemonade he had been casually consuming no longer provided him with the sureness he had previously possessed. She smiled at him, slowing her movements without ceasing. Now that he was closer he could see the sheen of sweat that dripped over her embroidered headband, giving her an appealing, unflattering glow.

'Could I buy you a drink?' She laughed, draping her hand over his arm and guiding him to the bar.

She leaned daintily over it to whisper her order to the bartender as Fredrick watched in a fascinated stupor.

'And for you?' Her eyes slid to his, a smile still gracing her face.

He mentally shook himself and ordered a gin. Fredrick and the lady waited in thunderous silence for their drinks to be made, as if carved into their surroundings. As much as he tried to distract himself, studying the thin beauty beside him proved more interesting than any of the fun-deprived patrons of the Cotton Club. She breathed heavily, her eyes flitted from person to person as she neglected to even attempt to remain still. Her small movements, always somehow to the beat (and never off-beat), intrigued Fredrick so much he barely noticed she had received her bright green drink until she was tugging on his arm once more.

'What's your name?' she asked breathlessly, stifling a spin as she gulped her elixir.

Fredrick reached over the bar to pick up his own drink, sipping it slowly, 'Fredrick.'

He hoped she could hear him over the music, but she simply frowned at the word and yet again latched herself onto his arm in order to guide him. Fredrick followed her, entranced by the energy emitted by her small form. She led him through the outlawed smog of the dance hall, into the stairwell and up again.

'There,' she declared, releasing him and twirling across the rooftop. Fear seized his heart as she dipped toward the night sky and he reached out to her from his spot.

Laughter echoed all the way back to him as she rose gracefully, 'Well, my name is–'

'Please, Miss, come away from the edge.' Fredrick moved closer, concerned as ever.

She looked behind her in shock, as if the prospect of tumbling to her death had only now occurred to her.

'Oh, why are you so scared, Freddy?' She giggled, offering him her hand. Bewildered, he took it and leaned down to kiss it softly.

Her breath caught in her throat as if, when she had put on her embellished black and teal dress, she had never imagined that anyone would kiss her hand.

'Oh my, Sir, you must think I'm some sort of lady,' she exclaimed, her hand remaining in his a moment longer.

'A lady I'd like to know better,' he stammered, his eyes caught in her carefully styled hairdo.

She giggled again, placing the hand he once held on her neck. Fredrick studied her as she turned, approaching the top of the fire escape.

'Now, please be careful over there.' He shuffled closer as she peered down into the scattered light of the street.

'So quickly,' she told him, 'it's over so quickly.' Fredrick had no clue what she meant, but she gave him no time to consider it.

'Oh Freddy, don't you want to dance with me?' she asked – her drink having evaporated while she was speaking.

'I would very much like to.' He returned her smile, placing his own drink several steps away from them.

He once again took her hand and clumsily pulled her closer to him. She placed her head on his shoulder as her slightly too-big nose squished into him. Fredrick was overwhelmingly certain that he didn't mind.

'Wouldn't the world be much nicer if we all saw it from someone's shoulder?' she breathed.

Fredrick was inclined to agree, he knew first hand how merciless life could be. Especially to those as unsuspecting as the tissue paper lady in his arms. He fancied that if it began to rain, she would wash away before his eyes.

'I suppose,' he agreed, taking comfort in her small frame for just a moment.

'It's so cruel sometimes. Like that horrible war all those men went to. All that fighting and where are they now? Right back where they started.' Fredrick pulled away slightly to look at her tear marked face.

'Well, the lucky ones are.' He gently wiped away the droplets, cradling her face in his hand. 'Maybe right back where they started is all they wanted?' he offered, gently spinning her away from him.

She continued to spin until she almost toppled over, carelessly extending her arms as she cried: 'Oh Freddy. I wish they hadn't fought so hard.' She stopped her pirouettes, stumbling still so she could watch the city morph.

She knew that the sun was beginning to rise and that, soon, she would have to end her tired party. Drink after drink, dance after dance. She knew then that none would compare to this dance with her Freddy.

'I know, Barbara. I know.'

She looked at him from across the rooftop. Beads of sunlight began to drip over her face, darkening the murky depths of her eyes as they met his.

'I'm scared, you know.' Within seconds, her pupils had

become unfocused and dreaming. He tilted his head gently, fearful a sudden movement would break her unanticipated mirage. 'I'm scared I'll never fall in love.'

Fredrick heard such honesty in her voice that he felt compelled to look away. The blonde girl sniffed and looked down at her hands. 'Maybe all that education and all of those books ruined me. Maybe now, my expectations are so high that I will never find love.' She tilted her head to the side.

'I've heard, Miss, that love rather prefers to find you.' He offered her a gentle smile and she released a sad puff of air.

'Oh yes, but I'm tired of waiting. My feet have traced this earth for almost two decades now – and they have been loud, hazy years.' Her shoulders slumped almost imperceptibly, so much so that Fredrick was proud he noticed.

'I have some thoughts, if… if you'd like to hear?' Her red lips split into a sincere smile, warming his heart.

'Oh Freddy, I would love nothing more.' She wandered over to him, extending her hand absent-mindedly.

He captured it, holding the porcelain softly. 'Well I think, you see, that maybe,' Fredrick studied her carefully painted nails to ground himself, 'everyone I know spends their time thinking they're lost. They all stroll past each other, too blinded by what they're looking for to notice what's around them. We're all so distracted.'

Fredrick was too frightened to look at her.

'When we cry, when we laugh and when we love it's as if we're filled with such… such…'

'Dissatisfaction.' Fredrick's focus jumped to the girl beside him in surprise, her entranced expression enough to make any person believe they were the sun to which she orbited.

'Yes.' He nodded.

'I think it's human nature,' her mouth was barely moving as she gazed at him, 'that is, it's human nature to focus on the future. Living in the moment is so enjoyable precisely because we don't realise we're doing it.' Her eyes closed and as she swayed lightly in the soft breeze, she took a few steps away from him.

'Sometimes I like to live in the past, though.' Her hand reluctantly fell from his as she faced the horizon.

'I do too.' Despite the humid night, Fredrick's palm felt oddly cold without her touch.

'I don't want the sun to rise.' He could hear the murmur clearly.

She floated forward, as if she could reach up and pull the curtains over the honeyed sky. A pigeon fluttered between them, startling her into facing him once more.

'I already miss you,' she told him. Fredrick offered her his arm in response.

She daintily swept over to him, her dress rippling gently in the wind. She returned her head to his chest and they began to sway to the beat of their unsteady breaths.

'All those poor women who never got their husbands back. I bet they would rather live in the past forever,' she lamented. 'Not me though, because you'll come back. Won't you Freddy?'

He turned his head, placing his hand on her jaw as she moved her head to look at him.

'Freddy? You'll be back, won't you?'

He stroked her cheek with his thumb. 'The war is over, Barbara.'

Her eyes glistened, threatening a tsunami. 'It can't be, you haven't come back yet.'

His face softened into sympathy.

She stopped swaying when a car horn sounded, thumping against the silence that had contained them. She withdrew from his sheltering hold and stormed a few steps away.

'No, no, no, no, no, no, no.' Fredrick watched her sadly. She sporadically spun to face him, her face composed carelessly and her arms slumped at her sides.

'I'm–' She cut off his words by crying out, once again turning away from him to focus on the building across from them.

'Barbara,' he warned. She didn't listen. She braced herself and began to run towards it.

A clip fell from her hair, causing a cascade of gold to surround her. Closer and closer. The side of the rooftop approached all too rapidly. Fredrick wanted to stop her. But right before the brink, she threw her hands out, grazing her skin as she skidded along the concrete. Knees crumpled beneath her, she froze and stared into the street at the awakening world. Two men yelled from below, causing commotion at the sight of her dangerous escapade. She frowned.

'Freddy.'

He took a step closer.

'You haven't come back yet, Freddy,' she insisted, twisting her head to look at him while remaining perched at the edge of the roof like a watchful stone lion.

'Barbara.'

She released a shuddering sob, turning her back on the wide world. She clutched her sides, staring through him while her hair blew wildly around her. She teetered haphazardly between this moment and the next.

'I'm not coming back.' Her breath hitched as his words hit her heart, the impact knocking her backwards.

As she began to fall, Fredrick ran to seize her hand. Her palms hit concrete and her torn fingers clutched at the building until they found something to grip. A man in overalls burst through the rooftop door, running past Fredrick to haul her up over the side. Through the panic surrounding her small frame, Barbara watched as Fredrick turned from her and began his journey back inside the dance hall. As she watched him retreat, she knew irrefutably that she would see him again.

But for now, he was gone.

The dawn had broken and her dance was over.

Thomas Tyrrell

Earthquake in Powys

Now and then, when you've got a job at a greenfield site out in the hinterlands and you've driven in your piles, laid your foundations, got the first floor of the house done and maybe a bit of the second or third, you'll come in bright and early one morning and find the whole lot shaken down to nothing but rubble and twisted rebar. And the security guard is babbling something about an earthquake — *an earthquake? in Wales?* — while the surveyor scratches his head and mutters something about the underlying geology or the fracking down in Porth. He eventually throws his hands up, gets on the phone to the client and suggests changing the site.

Ignore him. He doesn't know what he's talking about. Nine times out of ten, your root cause is dragons.

I saw it as recently as last April, pulling into the site to find the whole construction team standing around in a state of shock. We'd been working at it for nine months with another two years scheduled in — a really good, satisfying work commitment — and suddenly, it was like a giant had stepped on the entire project. The shining white McMansion / survivalist hideaway we'd been putting up for the secretive American client was lying at our feet like so much shattered Lego. The site office, a converted shipping container, had toppled over onto its side, and the interior was a hopeless wreck of dented filing cabinets, smashed computers, loose blueprints, paperwork and coffee cups. Meanwhile, the village I'd driven through a few miles back hadn't seen so much as a cracked window pane.

I went to find Rhys, the assistant foreman. He'd got his hard hat on and was up among the ruins, doing a quick damage assessment.

'Is it them, do you think? Under the earth?'

Rhys checked for anyone who might overhear. 'Most likely.'

'Salvageable?'

'We've lost the upper storeys, but the foundations look to have stood firm. Think we can continue. If someone can convince Howard and Williams to turn a blind eye to it.'

'Bloody hell, are they in today?'

'Back down in the car park. Last I heard, they were trying to get fifteen minutes with the client, to keep him up to date.'

'Oh, that's the last thing we need. You keep going up here. I'll see if I can get them off our backs.'

Thanks to the planning regs, we don't do that much greenfield building anymore. While I've been around a bit and seen a few things in my time, it was too much to expect a fancy foreign architect and a big city boy to understand how we did things up country. I was going to have to set them straight.

In the absence of the office, Howard Breckinridge, the architect, and William Williams, the construction manager, had put their laptop on the bonnet of Howard's Range Rover and were in the middle of an open-air Skype call. I watched them a moment, waiting for my chance to butt in. Howard had obviously headed up to the ruins without changing into overalls. He looked rumpled and dusty, and the wind kept catching his tie and blowing it over his shoulder. Williams, meanwhile, looked like he was going to lose his breakfast any minute. If this prestige project collapsed a bare nine months in, he'd be reckoning up the cost to his mortgage and his marriage, never mind his business. Sweat was coursing down from the rim of his hard hat.

'What do you mean, it's fallen down?!' Even through the tinny speakers of the laptop, the client's rage was palpable.

'There seems to have been some kind of… freak seismic event of some sort. We're not sure how…'

'There's a reason I decided not to build this project in New Zealand. I weighed the risk of a major natural disaster against a less resilient ecosystem and opted for your country. If you can't deliver…'

'May I cut in here, boys?' I asked, coming forward. Howard and Williams turned to me with the stricken faces of newlyweds surprised by objections at the altar.

'Ambrose Roberts,' said Williams in a low hiss, 'what in God's name do you think you're doing?'

'Just a moment of your time, sir,' I said, addressing the very bald, very rich, very famous face at the other end of the video call. 'This isn't an unknown phenomenon, in these parts. We have ways of dealing with it. But we do so in our own way, in our own time.' I took a deep breath. 'I'm going to need a closed site for the next twenty-four hours. No-one allowed in except on my say-so, and that includes these two. After that, there shouldn't be any more problems. You have my word on that.'

Just for a few seconds, I was standing under the scrutiny of one of the richest men in the world. MPs and Senators have spent thousands of pounds for exactly that kind of visibility.

'Get it done,' he said.

'Sir, I really must…' said Howard.

'If he can't do what he's promised, what have we lost? Twenty-four hours. Hardly a great over-run on a three-year project with two million in sunk costs already. Far less than relocating it to New Zealand. I'll expect a full update tomorrow morning. And Mr…'

'Roberts,' I supplied.

'Mr Roberts, I don't take kindly to people making a fool of me. Be sure you deliver, or I'll know the reason why.'

He cut the connection.

'You heard the client,' I said. 'Off the site. Now. I've got things to do.'

Howard glared at me and straightened his tie. 'Better come in tomorrow with a good appetite, Williams, because I'm going to roast your man for breakfast.' He turned and walked off.

Williams hung around, irresolute. 'What on earth was all that about? What have you got up your sleeve?' he asked.

'Ah, Billy, Billy,' I said, 'you're a good lad, but you're a city boy, when all's said and done. What we have to do up by here would only give you nightmares.'

'I've known you five years, Ambrose, I think I deserve a little…'

'No, I mean it. Go home and say you've got the day off. Play with the children. Show the wife a little romance. By the time you turn up tomorrow morning, it'll all be over.'

By now we'd all gathered around, the boys who knew what was coming next, and we were bulky enough to dissuade him from trying to order us about. He gave us a final puzzled look, but finally turned and climbed into the Range Rover. We watched as it turned out of the gates after Howard's BMW, and we kept on watching as the two cars climbed the lane and were finally lost over the hill.

'You boys know the drill,' I said. 'We dig. Clear the earth, get the JCBs up there. I'm going to make a few calls.'

They trickled in, one by one, as the digging went on. I'd

spread the word around, but I always got the feeling they would turn up even if I hadn't, drawn here like filings to a magnet or moths to a flame, drawn by a force beyond their ability to understand. Old men in yellowing shirts with faces like withered apples. Women of all ages, in estate cars or quad bikes, tracksuits or twin sets. Farmers and their border collies standing together and looking on with the same patient eyes. Families with normally rowdy kids, staring like they were hypnotised as the diggers went on bringing up the fine brown clay, scoop by scoop. One man, turning up late in the afternoon with his eleven-year-old son in tow, told me he'd come from as far away as London, the news dragging him through hundred-mile traffic jams and back over the border. All for the sake of bearing witness. We kept them behind barriers but allowed them to keep watching. It was traditional.

By the time afternoon was drawing in, we were ten feet down, and the site looked like an open cast mine in miniature. Eventually, we broke through the last layer of mudstone and the water started welling up.

'Pumps,' I said, and the hoses went down into the water. Engines began to hum.

We'd rigged up arc lighting so we could continue at night, but the wattage didn't satisfy the crowd, who drove their cars up to the barrier and left their headlights running, high beams lighting up every corner of the pit as the water slowly sank, exposing long-buried strata of limestone and marl.

As the water level sank, other shapes began to emerge. Murmurs ran through the crowd like disturbances in the air. What could have been a jag of rock began to look like an ear. A mound of mud started to resemble a torso — and then it was unmistakable. The water level sank and laid the creatures bare.

When first they started to stir, I felt all the hair on my body stand on end. Terror flared down my spinal cord — a terror nothing like the rational fears of my comfortable life, no, like coming face to face with a tiger, of being helpless before something fiercer, stronger, more powerful. If these creatures from under the earth turned on us, we had no way of resisting them. To them, we were nothing more than a mouthful of meat. For a moment, as the two draconian heads rose from the mud and regarded us with cold lizard-eyes, the question hung in the balance. Then they saw each other, and with roars of defiance, began to fight.

They always fight. No-one knows why, or what for, or what feud could last for so many ages, sleeping under the earth. We watched silently, intensely, following every blow, never making a sound. All of us, having borne that reptilian stare, were wary of drawing its attention again.

One was a muddy brown colour, paler at the head and ruddier at the tip of the tail. The other, larger creature was blue, speckled with yellow. Both, at different times, seemed to be winning. At first the brown one was on top, sinking its teeth into its rival's neck, then the blue one was uppermost, clawing its foe.

The more mystically minded of the spectators — those who've been drawn to more than one encounter — say that each fight presages a conflict yet to come, ever since Merlin predicted the fate of the British and the Saxons. I don't know what to say about that, other than if it's true, every fight I've seen predicts a bloody stalemate, if not a suicide pact.

Eventually, they broke apart, streams of blood gushing from their flanks to pool in the mud. They eyed each other, their great bodies heaving with exertion like treetops in a gale, before they charged. The smack of their collision was thunderous. Fangs and claws sunk deep in one another's flesh, they toppled into the mud — and lay still.

We watched them for at least half an hour. Neither stirred. The old terror retreated, slinking back down into the base of the spine. Perhaps never to be set loose again. There can't be many of them left under the earth.

For the first time in over an hour, we raised our eyes and looked around, and the world was ours again. An ordinary place of environmental protection, planning regulations, concrete, tarmac and cement. An American CEO would live here, perhaps for two weeks in a year or less. Never to guess at what had lain dreaming below him since time immemorial.

The spectators looked at each other with lost, wondering eyes, shuddered, hugged themselves, gathered their things and turned back to their cars. The show was over.

'Fill it in,' I said, and the bulldozers began to lumber forward.

Death Junction

Death Junction is the nickname for a place
        where five roads meet in Roath, a place
        all Cardiff people come to know.
There, Crwys, Albany and City roads
        combine in such a crazy whirl
        of drivers and pedestrians
as seems to justify the name. Few guess
        how, near four hundred years ago,
        John Lloyd and Philip Evans met
their deaths, hung, drawn and quartered, on this spot
        all for the crime of practicing
        the Roman faith in times of plots
and paranoia; martyrdom in this
        as other cases put them on
        the fast-track to their sainthoods. Now
upon their lonely execution ground,
        a place where nothing stood, except
        the gallows and the empty heath,
the traffic roars away in five directions.
        Only a plaque above the bank
        preserves the martyrs' sanctity
in face of modern apathy, but still,
        sometimes I like to picture them
        drifting above the traffic lights,
their thankless miracles primed for the kids
        the white van never clips, who'll reach
        the pavement and stroll on without
thinking to offer up a thought or prayer.

Jonathan Macho

Wrong Number

The Upper Cwmtwrch Satanist Society (or *Cymdeithas yr Sataniaeth Cwm-twrch Uchaf* – everything has to be bilingual in Wales) met every Saturday afternoon. It was the sixth day, the last day God ever tried for us, and also everybody was off work. Well, almost everybody, but Aled the butcher had his son take over in the shop every other week, so that had to do.

Yes, the Upper Cwmtwrch Satanist Society met every Saturday afternoon. Except for this week. This week, they were meeting on a Tuesday evening. This was for myriad reasons, not the least of which being everyone was working that afternoon. Moreover, it was no ordinary Tuesday. It was, in fact, the most important Tuesday since the Heavens were set in motion. Everybody was coming. Except for Aled, but his son had something on.

It was a grey day, the kind that threatened rain even after the rain had stopped. This was nothing unusual, and that was probably the point. If the sky had burned red with unnatural or even explainable purpose, it could alert someone, somewhere that unimpeachable change was coming. Instead, there was that tang in the air, the taste of water that was still figuring out its travel arrangements, and that splash underfoot from the rest that had gotten in early. Not welcome weather, just expected.

It was from this dreek and drear that Howell welcomed

the last members with a warm smile and a reminder to wipe their feet. He shook Mr Hughes by the hand and asked Mrs Hughes how little Morgan was doing in school. He didn't have to tell them where to go; they were long time attendees and dear friends. Hanging their coats in the cloak room, Howell couldn't help but grin as he followed them through to cheers and greetings from all who had gathered. He hadn't even told them the news yet. They were just this lovely, and Dark Lord knows they'd taken this sudden change in plans on the chin. He was lucky to have them, every one.

'…and so the pilot says: Upper Cwmtwrch or Lower Cwmtwrch? Haha!'

Well, almost every one. The grin soured at the sound of that punchline, of nobody laughing but the man delivering the joke.

'Do you not have other jokes, Leonard?' Mr Hughes asked as he took a seat by the dining table. 'Every time with that joke, mun! Every time!'

Leonard shrugged in that way that made you want to throw something at him. 'You can't beat the classics.'

'Can you though?' Gwen called from the kitchen, mid-biscuit run. 'I'd like to give it a bloody good try!'

Everybody laughed. Except for Leonard. Leonard frowned.

Oh, Leonard. Howell often wrestled with what it was that bothered him so much about Leonard. He didn't think it was because he was Saes; he hoped he was a bigger man than that. In Satan's eyes all are equally damned, after all. It wasn't that he never brought snacks, or that he spoke up at every council meeting, or that he loved using the word 'Actually…' whenever he contradicted you. It was more… primal.

Leonard just took all the joy out of Satanism.

Well, he wouldn't spoil today. Howell cleared his throat

75

before Leonard could 'Actually…' anybody. 'Right, settle down then. I have called this meeting of the Upper Cwmtwrch Satanist Society for a very special reason. I know it's put a lot of you out, and I know we all wish Aled could be here…'

There was an: 'Ere-ere!' from the back.

'…but I know it'll all be worth it when you understand what lays before us tonight. The importance of today's date can't have gone unnoticed to all of you. June 6th, in the year of our Enemy 2006. This is the only opportunity in our lifetimes, in a hundred lifetimes, for us to convene on the night of the number of the Beast.'

Palpable awe filled the room. Mugs rattled. Breaths were taken in, sharply. Bryn from the shop managed a 'Bloody hell.'

'Actually, that's wrong,' Leonard said.

Howell could have killed him. It took a lot to get the Upper Cwmtwrch Satanist Society excited these days. There were very few dark ministrations about. Tea and biscuits took up the majority of their meetings; tea, biscuits and the odd friendly touch-rugby game with the Lower Cwmtwrch Witches Guild. Yes, they would read texts and share ideas about what it all meant, but this was the first time in forever that they could get involved, get excited about their faith again. And there was bloody Leonard, spoiling it as only he could.

'What?' Howell said, through gritted teeth.

'666 is not the number of the Beast,' Leonard insisted. 'Theologians have doubted it for some time now. Earlier texts have the number at 616.'

There was silence.

'Bollocks,' came a cry from the settee.

'Yeah, everyone knows 666,' Gwen said through digestives. 'Iron Maiden innit.'

'Look,' Leonard said, 'I'm just saying that if we want to be accurate...'

'Besides which,' Mr Hughes cut in, 'Howell here has gone to a lot of trouble for us. He always does. The least we owe him is to hear him through, right?'

There were shouts of approval and the odd clinked mug. His Society. Howell knew then and there that he couldn't hope for a better bunch to do this with. He was feeling a little emotional actually. Pulling himself together, not wanting to put a dampener on the special day, he opened his chest of drawers and retrieved a glossy, brown-bound and yellow-paged book. Heaving it to the dining table, he let it fall in front of the assembled faithful.

'Within these ancient pages,' he said, plumbing the depths of his reverence for maximum effect, 'there is a passage that, if spoken aloud among true believers on the day of the number of the Beast, will call out into the dark and that will be... answered.'

'Bloody, bloody hell...' Bryn had to sit down.

'I should think so,' Howell said, beaming. 'Who's up for it then?'

Everyone was. Of course they were. Even Leonard, although he grumbled to anyone who would listen that there was no way it was going to work and this would just prove his point anyway, so... Howell gave them all a minute to put their robes on (they always brought them but they tended to trip over the hems if they weren't careful, so they were saved for special occasions) and got to work lighting candles all through the house, flicking off lights, closing the curtains, and letting out the cat. It was all very atmospheric. Gwen even *oooh*-ed when she got back from the loo.

There was total silence as Howell found the passage. You could feel it, like the pressure outside, that tang of promised rain; something was coming. The candles flickered, as candles were supposed to do in times like these. It was all Dai Jenkins could do not to sneeze.

The words were like nothing they had heard before, as far from Welsh as Welsh was from English, with an alphabet that a human tongue couldn't do justice to. The air went from tasting of ozone to burning with brimstone. The candles went out, one after the other to begin with, then all at once. Dai was too scared to sneeze now.

Howell finished. It was pitch black, so still, so quiet. Seconds passed. Too many. Leonard was going to be so damn smug—

And then the table burst into flames, a crimson gout that scorched the floors and the ceilings but left the gathered people unharmed, and when the fire had died as suddenly as it appeared, the Devil stood in the living room.

It was bizarre; he looked at the same time nothing like Howell had expected, and exactly as he felt he should look. Redder than anything he had ever seen (and as a Welshman, he knew red), the figure before him shone, lighting the room in crimson by simply being in it. Of course there were horns, curved and ridged, but there were no cloven hooves after all, no wings, no tail. Just those eyes, burning gold, and that smile, broader than Howell's, growing broader all the time.

'Oh, you did it,' he breathed. His voice was deep and rich, clear to all even though he spoke softly. 'You humans actually did it. I kept the faith and I was rewarded.' He laughed. Some of them jumped. 'They all told me it was a long shot, but I said hey, if you're given a number you might as well use it, right? All you humans do is numbers; you love numbers up here…' He stretched, cracking his neck, before snapping it to look at Howell. 'Where are we? Which of you was it, in the end?'

'...Uh, uh, Upper Cwmtwrch, lord,' he said through the driest mouth he'd ever had.

'Wales? But that's perfect!' The Devil was ecstatic. This scared the group more than they were expecting. 'I gave you my son, you know. How Biblical is that? Myrrdin Emris! How did you say it... Merlin! Great kid, went on his own path, but you have to respect their choices don't you?'

'Actually...'

It was like the Ice Age started in a split second. Somehow the crimson glow turned cold. The Satanists of Upper Cwmtwrch ripped their eyes from their calling, their destination, the impossible made flesh before them, and looked instead to a thoroughly unimpressed Leonard.

'Merlin is a myth, not a real historical figure. He was inserted into an apocryphal history by Geoffrey of Monmouth. It's speculated that he's based on Myrddin Wyllt, a prophet and madman.'

'Is he now?' the Devil murmured with the loudest murmur they'd ever heard. 'I'll make sure to tell him.'

'And besides which, this proves it,' Leonard said to the group at large, completely bypassing the Beast before him. As his eyes moved on, the room somehow grew colder.

'Proves what?' the Devil said with admirable calm.

'That you're not the real Devil.'

There was the longest silence. The red glow came from outside now, like the sky actually was burning red with unnatural purpose.

'Really? How did you reach that conclusion?'

'The number's wrong.'

Howell wanted to say something, anything, to distance himself and his friends from this spectacular suicide, but it was impossible to speak in the face of such stupidity. Somehow, Leonard had managed to be the most alarming thing in the room that night. More alarming still, however, was what the Devil did next.

He laughed and clapped Leonard on the back. 'Oh my dear acolyte, the number doesn't matter!' Suddenly the glow was warm and interior again. The Devil's words could hardly be heard over the sighs of relief. 'That's not how it works. I am a creature of faith, a poisonous thought germinating from the beginning of what you understand to be time, an abstract, liminal thing. The numbers work not because of some cosmic code, some written law, God...' He winced. 'Forbid. They work because of the meaning you imbue them with. They work because you believe they will.'

'But I don't.'

Howell was going mad. There was no other explanation. The Devil was frowning at Leonard now. 'What?'

'I don't believe the numbers worked,' he stated. 'I don't believe you.'

The howl of agony that filled the room was like nothing heard in millennia. The impossible flame, now burning sickly green, swamped them again but this time, when it had died down, the Upper Cwmtwrch Satanist Society were alone. The smell of brimstone lingered, and the furniture was all scorched black. The only white in the room was a pile of ash that sat next to Leonard on the exact spot the Devil had stood moments earlier.

'What did you do?' Howell rasped as soon as the words would come.

'Fear not child,' said the most beautiful voice he had ever heard. 'He hath saved the world.'

The curtains flung themselves back, revealing an impossible light filling the Tuesday night sky. Standing there, framed perfectly in the window, were two men in long flowing robes and with feathered wings tucked behind their backs.

'You have done creation a great service, Leonard of the Upper Cwmtwrch Satanist Society,' one of them said.

'By confronting the Devil with thine own stout refusal at this, his moment of greatest potency,' the other continued with a flourish, 'thou hast un-believed him from this celestial sphere, severing his connection with yon precious Earth... forever.'

After the latest in a long line of stunned silences, Gwen yelled: 'Oh, nice one Leonard!'

'Hey, don't start!' Leonard said, finally seeming to notice the many furious eyes on him. 'Don't tell me you believe this nonsense too?'

Nobody was sure what to say.

'Come on guys.' Leonard sounded like he was talking to toddlers. 'I told you. 666 isn't the real number of the Beast, so that wasn't the real Devil, so these are obviously not real angels. Q.E.D.'

'Wait, hang on,' the first angel said.

'Truly, you know not what you do,' the other added.

'I don't know what's going on here,' Leonard said, the first thing he'd said all night which everyone agreed upon, 'but I do know that I am still right.'

The light outside started to flicker. The angels looked worryingly worried.

'Thaumiel, say something; you're the one with the words!'

The more verbose of them stepped forward. 'Leonard of Upper Cwmtwrch, if thou continuest down this path, thou take Heaven's balm and God's mercy from all who—'

'Actually I'm from Kent,' Leonard said, 'and *continuest* isn't a word.'

Thaumiel staggered backwards. His friend stepped up to replace him. 'Look human, if you don't quit this, you will un-believe us too, and mankind will be cut off from Paradise forever. Think for a minute, will you?'

'I do think,' he replied simply, completely still in the heart of a storm. 'I think I'm right.'

'His pedantry has power beyond possibility!' Thaumiel screamed.

'Lord above I hate you,' the other angel said with feeling.

There was a roar like a broken organ, played backwards and out of key, a wrenching screech that shook everything everywhere. And then they were gone.

Howell's room was back to normal, dining table included, but his book wasn't there. Some of the society were crying, most were sitting, none could look at each other. They all knew that this was their final meeting. It had been lovely while it lasted, but they had wiped their Lord from creation, not to mention the opposition, so there seemed little point now. They all felt grey, grey like the sky outside, grey like it promised to be tomorrow, and the next day, and the next.

Howell looked at Leonard. His eyes burned as his Master's had, back when they existed. 'I don't believe you.'

Leonard laughed. 'Nice try, but it won't work on me.'

Howell lunged at him.

Sidney Wollmuth

Traces of Water in Wilmington, North Carolina

It's time to slather tart
sunscreen on our
elbows and don
chunky
hoops
that clack
when we skate.
This sunstroked morning
begs
us to wash our teeth with
bubble gum paste, reflecting
on water-stained dreams —
the lure of the ocean, how
unrequited lust can be
sometimes.

We plan hammock
hazes while we walk
down sidewalks, Air
Pods ditched for gooey
gossip, sneakers swapped
for sandals that sing
of sand. Water bottles swing

from ringed fingers, from
shiny belt buckles — the liquid
tilting, swaying, beautiful even
after it's been filtered.

Not much work gets done
in our classes; we are too
busy chasing down
waves. It is easy
to forget the storm,
the devastation, the dangers
that can come from such
lures.
We live in a bubble of
blissful forget: sculpting water
into our lab reports, threading
it into our films, rationalising it
in our poetry.

At night, we lay in the thick of
it, our skin burning as the
temperature drops. We clutch
each other's wrists, a sort
of reminder, an almost
promise, and we look up
at the sky. The beach is dark
enough to make out the stars
and so we stare, holding each
other tightly so that we don't
float away.

Eluned Gramich

Visa: Family Route

Holding hands in yoga class
our swollen stomachs swaying
the Indonesian lady tells me that her visa
will run out three days after
the birth of her son.

How to put on paper my love for you,
Foreigner husband, the warmth of your breath
on the top of my head as we sleep
your dark eyes when you say
Eu te amo muito, muito.

You used to dream of home
now we dream together of the
home office: homelessness, hostile
spectres haunting our hearts
as we try to carry on as if
nothing is being decided.

It would be easier if you were not
but then I would never have heard *Cartola,*
Chico, the *sambistas*, spirits of the *Candomblé*
I would never have learned to eat salmon
with passionfruit, black beans with orange slices.

The world is a windmill
says the singer from your country.
We hear about a Nigerian woman
married for two decades
denied, deported, dismissed
as she fought to remain with her family.

They ask for evidence
but what evidence can I give?
Invite them here so they can watch
how you cook for me, how you study *Cymraeg*,
how you sing to the baby at night, even though she is still
inside me. *Meu amor, pode me ouvir*?

They want to know about money. Fine.
But how to put on the form
the way you phone your parents before you buy
the simplest thing for yourself
unsure of whether you deserve a shirt
or a pair of trousers not falling apart?

Pão de queijo, hot from the oven,
sweet peanuts, golden *dendé* oil, *fy nghariad*,
suddenly, I am no longer your wife but your
sponsor and you, *meu amor*, are my dependent
still waiting for a stranger in London to decide
if we are in love.

Megan Angharad Hunter

Wings

I was ten years old when I started growing wings.

Standing in my first bra (a gentle, purple thing peppered with daisies) in front of the full-length mirror in Mam's room, I remember noticing the crack first: top-left corner of the mirror, as long as my palm is wide. Like a black thread in clear water. And I wondered, I wondered how it had happened. I wondered if it had been there all along and I just hadn't noticed because my brain feels like it's been replaced by a damp, scrunched-up dishcloth sometimes. I remember tracing my finger as slow as summer along that crack, wanting to (not wanting to), needing to (not needing to) turn around and see it: the calamus (back then I had no idea what the tail of a feather's spine was called, but some quick Googling on my phone gave me its name) protruding through the freckled skin covering my left shoulder blade.

I swung my arm over my right shoulder – neck muscles aching as I looked back at my reflection – and held the calamus between my index finger and thumb. Then I pulled. Quickly.

I remember my teeth clacking as I locked them together to suppress a scream; and there it was. The feather. The first feather. My first feather, its barbs (those are the feather's filaments, or so Wikipedia says) heavy with blood. And beneath the red – yellow? Green? More red? – I can't remember. I can't remember the colour. But I do remember pulling my school polo shirt back over my head and charging out of Mam's room, along the corridor, and dropping the feather into the toilet before pulling on that ridiculous old chain Mam insisted on keeping after we moved here and watching the feather disappear in a whirlpool of pinkish toilet water. I remember feeling like I was being pulled down with it, or a part of me at least. The part of me that mattered; the living part of me. My heart, maybe. Again, I can't really remember.

Then I pulled a yellow velvet scrunchie from my wrist to tie my hair back before throwing up.

When my fingers had stopped shaking like I had two minutes left to tie down an A-Level essay exam, I wiped my mouth and nose with my hands before leaning over the sink to wash the blood from my index finger and thumb. I think I scrubbed for five minutes at least, my fingertips red and swollen and wrinkled when I finally closed the tap, the tangy scent of Aloe Vera soap so thick I could taste it.

And I thought that was it; I could've imagined the feather, and my heart was safely deposited in the ocean somewhere, or wherever toilet water goes. Mam didn't even notice that my fingers were sore the next day, that I was eating the M&S microwaved green curry with my left hand.

And school was school. Until year 7 that is; secondary school was a chorus of corsets and crudely painted masks until I saw her; the sun wrapped in skin.

We were in the canteen. I was sitting with Seren and Olivia, who were talking about beauty vloggers or something. She was sitting alone. She was alone but she didn't look lonely and I was jealous of that. I wonder if she knew that she didn't look lonely. I wonder if she knew that someone was jealous of her. I've always been too scared to ask because I think I'm the only person in the world who's selfish enough to want to be the subject of envy. I remember watching her eat (in the least stalker-y way imaginable), and I could tell that it was causing her physical pain not to screw up her face as she ate the rubbery sausage and watered-down mash on the greasy plastic tray in front of her, and I didn't realise that my designated corset and mask had been suffocating me until I reached for my first iPhone the next morning to turn off the alarm and felt it again. Like an old recurring nightmare that soft lullabies and night-lights should've safely tucked away for ever.

Luckily, Mam had an early shift that morning, so I removed my pyjama top and turned my back on the mirror. I remember breathing. Closing my eyes. Turning my head. Then opening them, fast, like ripping a plaster away. Or like plucking a feather.

When I remember it now, they must've looked beautiful but intangible, like two rainbows had decided to ditch stripes for once and pour from my shoulders in whirlpools. But when I opened my eyes that morning, I couldn't see the colours – or refused to, it's difficult to tell – I could only see the world as it fell away and landed, crumpled at my feet, as significant as discarded orange peel.

And I remember thinking: is this what other girls do? Do they condemn their wings too? Do other girls even have wings? Or do they condemn their underdeveloped breasts and cellulite and pot bellies when they look in the mirror?

After that I remember grabbing a pair of kitchen scissors from downstairs and cut two holes into the back of my school rucksack, big enough to fit them, to hide them. I swung my bag onto my shoulders and crammed them through each hole, one after the other, before turning my back to Mam's mirror again and smiling, breathless. So breathless, I could've still been corseted and masked just like everyone else.

I can't try to deny that no-one knew because they didn't say anything; they didn't say anything because they knew. Not to my face, anyway. Not when I was in the same room or anything. Not even in P.E. lessons where my wings couldn't have been more conspicuous as they brushed against the cold concrete walls of the changing room and feathers drifted onto mouldy tiles that might've been white, once.

But I knew. I knew they talked when I wasn't there – I mean, how could they not? I would've talked if I were them. I would've laughed and sneered and pointed. I would've ripped out a feather or two to study them under the microscopes in Bio. I tried to do that myself more than once and even considered cutting them loose from my shoulders too, but I've always been a bit of a coward and have very low pain tolerance, so I never did. All I could ever do was stand in front of Mam's mirror whenever she was out, turn my head to look over my shoulder, and reach my hands back to touch them.

*

I know it's weird and creepy to recollect, but I can remember the first time we touched.

We were passing in the modern languages corridor; she was walking towards the toilets at the end I think and I was walking to Spanish. We were parallel and I remember thinking about GCSE Maths and learning this rule about parallel lines: they can never touch. Ever. Forever running alongside one another but never crossing, however close they might become – and I remember thinking that I was breaking that rule, a Maths rule, a universal Maths rule; I was mocking Maths as I de-paralleled my path and squeezed my shoulder to hers to avoid a whack from someone's heavy rucksack, and as we touched, I think my capillaries abandoned capacity as the blood within them became rivers as wide and bustling as a city and I remember reeling my veins back just in time to turn around and see her disappear behind someone's ponytail, just in time to notice something white hiding beneath the hair at the back of her head: a cochlear implant.

The first three thoughts that occurred to me were born from nothing but ignorance and my stomach turns inside out as I remember those thoughts now:

1. She sits alone in the canteen because she has no friends.
2. She has no friends because she can't talk.
3. She can't talk because she's deaf.

Of course, none of these assumptions were true. This I learned on a Halloween night.

*

We were both very original: she was a bedsheet ghost and I was a sexy, Primark-bought devil. I think I still have those red sequined horns in a box under my bed somewhere. I remember arriving at Spoon's with these 4 other devils, who I haven't spoken to in years apart from the occasional Birthday greeting on Facebook timelines. We had boarded the 7:04pm train to the closest town that had a Wetherspoon's and – just like every other 6th former within a twenty-mile radius – packed into the pub as if by some telepathically-notified ritual.

I remember watching the precipitation of our breath slithering down the windows in rugged ribbons. We were everywhere: swaying on the sticky carpet and leaning against tables agleam with grease and yet, I noticed her immediately. After all, she was the only skin-wrapped sun in the room.

Her sheet was draped over the back of a chair when I

noticed her, talking amongst a group of boys whose names I don't remember, gesticulating fiercely like she was trying to conjure an elephant from thin air. Then one of the other devils thrust a radiation-blue pitcher into my arms and we drank until we could raise the plastic jugs upside down above our heads. I remember thinking that it looked like the sky was bleeding on us.

I don't remember much else between then and the toilets at Roguey's. But I do remember seeing her again on the dancefloor at Rogue Palace, the only nightclub in town. Roguey's has thirty-year-old male virgins, perpetually sticky floors and is often misnamed as 'Shithole' but they've also got a borderline unhealthy Abba obsession and 3-4-1 Sourz on Wednesday nights, so the place was unavoidable on Halloween.

I remember watching her dance in full ghost attire, jumping repeatedly on an invisible trampoline to this trippy remix of *Take a Chance on Me*

and i remember

maybe i think i don't i can't remember i can remember i can

shit

I remember kissing her in a plastic-walled cubicle, the cold metal of her septum ring on my cheek like a gunshot that I couldn't cower from.

In between throwing up and wiping our mouths with the last three sheets of toilet paper, I asked stupid questions like *how are you able to talk* and *will you still hear me if I turn around* and *do you still like music* and *are your other senses heightened*.

And then, without any warning, the apocalypse occurred: an earthquake banged against the cubicle door and tycoon laughter flowed along the ground to pool at our feet and her hand slipped from mine like she'd been carried away in a flood and she thrust the rusty lock open and disappeared without looking back and and all I did all I did was sit there, the moisture on the floor seeping through my skirt and brand-new slutty underwear I got on sale from Topshop.

I can't remember much else, but I do remember noticing them through the thin material of her crop top – wings. Like mine. I also remember the way noticing them made me feel, like I was standing in an empty field under a blue sky on a mountain somewhere, or like I was an empty field under a blue sky on a mountain somewhere.

I sent her an instant message: *"sorry x"* on Snapchat, and after she opened the message without a reply for a few torturous hours, she answered.

*

We've been communicating strictly on Snapchat since then.

"1A*, an A and a C" she says. *"I'm going!!"*. She's added a shooting star emoji to the message.

Even though I've somehow passed all my A Levels, I won't follow her. I can't. I've known for years that uni isn't for me; vintage clothes and books heavier than my head and toilet-sized bedrooms and clubbing until my skin's almost as bruised as my bank account. I haven't told her yet, but I think I want to learn sign language and become a teacher's assistant specialising in deaf kids. I've already applied for a job at a local primary school.

"I want to see you" I text.

"Me too" she answers.

"i cant do this" I say. My fingers are shaking so I have to type slowly like I'm drunk.

"I know" she says. *"It's ok."*

And we both know it's not. It's not okay.

And even though I'm here, I can see her there at the train station, wings tearing through the heavy threads of her vintage Urban Outfitters jumper. As she steps towards the door of the train she realises that she can fly there, she can fly to uni if she wants to. She realises she has that choice.

And even though I'll be here, I'll see her there on Instagram, her wingspan so wide she's dwarfing the dancefloor of the underground hipster nightclub (like she's been brandishing them all along), and I think I'll still feel the whisper of her feathers as they glide along my skin, gently, slowly, like precipitation dripping down a window at Spoon's. I think

maybe i think i don't i can't i can i can

shit

I think I'll still feel them, even through the screen of my phone.

Kathryn Tann

Common Gorse

The grass was stiff with salt and the rabbit droppings were all rolling dry. On either side of her were swathes of yellow. Gorse blooms whenever it likes, sometimes the odd cluster, occasionally in brilliant constellations – even in winter. That day the sky was full of indecision, but when the sun warms its yellow buds, gorse can fill the air with coconut. Get close and you can smell sweet cardamom, vanilla.

She had wanted to buy some flowers for mum that morning, but none had any reduced labels. She only had the ten pound note for the food shop. She needed her own few coins for the bus. She couldn't get the pink carnations, or even a bar of chocolate this week, but she could go to the sea.

The bus from town looped around every hour in winter, and if Tony the driver dropped her off at the car park for the stacks, he would make sure to stop again on the next circuit – even in February. So she could leave her shopping on the bus with him, walk to the cliffs, and spend almost forty minutes with the waves. Then onto the bus again to ride the last two stops to home. This made doing the Saturday shop much more interesting, even in February. She had a hidden perch, away from the main path and a short scramble down – she knew every hold by heart. Scuffing more scrapes into the toes of mum's old boots, she made her way along the sheep track, onto the rocks, and sat.

Waves always grow in sets of seven, she remembered him telling her. He said the seventh wave is always the largest, and then they start getting smaller again, like the moon when it's finished being full.

The sea was churning, but not quite stormy, and froth was gathering into the first waves of a new cycle. Her spot was sheltered. Being between rocks meant the sounds below were cupped to her, either side, like a pair of hands. She listened for a while, watching the water, and coming to the same conclusion – the closest colour to the February sea that she could think of, was the cut edge of a pane of glass. Old, thick glass: the deep teal you only see when you look at it from the side.

He would bring them both to the stacks when they were really young. He would make her hold onto his hand because she was smaller than her brother. The sea wind would make them tired and rosy, and they would sleep on the short drive home. They never climbed down to this particular spot though; this was hers. Her own version of the cliffs.

Her eyes swung with the waves. When she watched and listened for a while, she felt that pull. *L'appel du vide*, he used to say, puffed with adult knowledge. And though she hadn't a clue when she was young, now she knew exactly what it meant. The cliffs just there were sheer, they didn't stagger down like some. If she jumped, there'd be no obvious way out. The sea was restless, building up at third or fourth, and with her clothes heavy and the endless undulations, how would she lift herself? No footings were free from certain clawing waves. Yet something about that colour teal looked deeply tempting. Her thoughts fell into the sea this way a number of times. She watched a splay of seaweed flung between crests, just under the surface, rise and fall and disappear. She imagined the view from down there, imagined watching the rock face rise and fall and disappear, imagined gasps of wind and water shudder down her throat.

When they were older they came alone. Her big brother and her. They used to scour these stacks for old army bullets. The area was a firing range on certain days, used for practice, leaving bright turquoise treasure hidden along the coastline. They were coppery when really fresh, but most often they were that brilliant turquoise. The pair of them would crawl and climb and reach their small wrists into cracks. The best ones were lifted out of sandy pockets, still smooth and streamlined, still pointy – the ones which must have simply slowed and dropped. Sometimes the bullets needed prising out – the ones mangled by the rocks, splayed open while they were still fast and hot. They called those shrapnel. The only ones they left behind were the rusty ones: staining the rock, furredup, fat and orange. She wondered how many of those were welded to the bottom of the sea.

The next wave was swelling, gathering foam and voice. It closed onto the rocks, filling porous holes and dragging streams of salt water, like springs, back into the frosted green. The surface was squirming with all that froth, webs of it always moving and growing and dissolving. Each time the sun glanced over the water, greyish-bluish-green became emerald, and when the sharp rocks broke the emerald, it turned to shining crystal.

She and her brother would head home with weighted pockets, darting, giddy, amongst the scented gorse and past the sign – the one which looked like a cheese grater with all its bullet holes – the one which said: 'DANGER – PERYGL – DO NOT TOUCH ANY MILITARY DEBRIS IT MAY EXPLODE AND KILL YOU – PEIDIWCH CYFFWRDD UNRHYW WASTRAFF MILWROL FE ALL FFRWYDRO A'CH LLADD'. There was an image on the sign of something shattered, with black streaks beaming out of it. At home they would line their bullets up on the windowsill, ordered by size, then smoothness, and make a pile for the prettiest shrapnel pieces.

They would barely notice the waves when they were bullet-hunting. Their eyes would be pinned down, they would forget the house, the dusk, and the bike-ride home. It was always competitive, see. A treasure hunt.

She watched a sixth wave meet the cliff and reach up, branching into a thousand glistening fingers, slowing at its height, pausing, before dropping and showering the sea with a sound that made her shiver.

Sometimes, in the summer, they had come to the stacks together. All four of them. They walked further east near the beaches, and jumped from above a specific cave and into the blue. In the summer it was more blue than green, and bright and glowing. There they could climb out onto the natural steps, the sea lapping happily at their feet. Mum would be sat, straw-shaded, further up, laughing and squealing with them when they jumped.

In February the sea was glass-edge green, and apparently deadly. A seventh wave rolled into the headland on her right. She could feel it: it rumbled. A huge mass of water knocking the wind out of the rocks, felt in the earth and rising in the air. She used to wonder if the cliffs might be tired of the sea, heaving its weight against them, over and over. But she had decided that the sea seemed tired too, of its ceaseless advance and retreat. She imagined the sea speaking with the cliffs, as old friends would, apologising – wearily. The cliffs would understand.

He had driven them to the cliffs three days before he left. It was stormy and they had wanted to hear it roar. The Dragon, Dad had called it. And she remembered it well. When waves pitched into a certain cliff, air was forced up through hidden cracks, sour and angry – with a sound to make little children cry. They stayed safe on the grass on Dad's instructions, and waited for the right wave. But it never came. The crack must be blocked up with rocks and rubble, Dad had told them. A shame. Two and a half days later he had driven away from them. And in the car, her brother too – on Dad's instructions.

The wind was getting colder and her eyes were streaming. There were thirteen minutes until the bus came back, and it took nine to reach the car park. She couldn't wait for the next loop round – there was mince in one of the shopping bags, and Mum would wonder. Climbing away from the quiet edge, she came back to the path. She dug her hands, suddenly noticing their sting, into her raincoat pockets. They'd been gone four years to the day. Four years without a word or a bit of help for her and Mum. Thank goodness it was Grandma's house; they mainly had to think of food. And then, in February, they felt it most: that's when the heating got expensive.

Four years. Tomos didn't have to go too. She noticed her pocketed hand rolling something smooth and cold, dotted with grippy rubber. She smiled when she realised what it was. The sleek little penknife that she would stow in her raincoat pocket when she was younger. That morning she had picked this coat off the hook because her winter puffa was soaked through, and then squashed three layers of sleeves into the tight arms. This penknife had been a birthday present from her brother, bought from their favourite dodgy corner shop. It had a blunt blade, tiny sharp scissors, and an unused file, all tucked neatly inside. She had loved this penknife with the childish heart of an adventurer, and later she had used it with the frustration of a girl, panicked and sad, who didn't know how to make things better.

Turning the metal between her fingers, she followed the

path away from the stacks and through the gorse. The air was biting harder but the sun had made a more decisive appearance. It reached across the prickly swathes of yellow and brightened it, quite suddenly, into a smiling mass. She stopped. She could smell it – the coconut and sweet something. She stepped and craned in closer. Deep inhale. The cardamom. Vanilla.

She took out the penknife and, digging a grubby nail into one of the notches – she could remember which it was – eased out the tiny pair of scissors. She tried to pinch a small branch, but the spikes were formidable. She slid the Velcro cuffs of her coat over her knuckles and tried again. After a few scrams and three successful sprigs, she unwrapped her scarf and wound it around the bunch, making an odd-looking bouquet and padding the pricks from her hands. She did this while walking quickly – only six minutes until Tony would be there and gone again.

'Hiya love. What you got there? Found something?'

'Oh, no. It's just some flowers. For Mum. You know.'

'In February?'

The doors unfolded behind her with a clatter.

'Actually, they're gorse flowers.' She felt embarrassed, wanted to clutch them tighter but a sharp prick to the thumb reminded her against it.

'Blimey. Never thought of picking those.' He reached out and gave her arm a rub. 'It's a fab idea. She'll love 'em.'

Taking her seat on the trundling bus, she balanced the bundle on her lap. She hoped the coconut smell would fill their little kitchen and – there was a jar just emptied of the last scrape of jam this morning – she would put them in that.

The wind-swept gorse would make Mum smile. It was a beautiful colour, that yellow.

Cynan Llwyd

Cardiff c.2100

It's dark. I fumble and listen,
but my mind is silent. I reach,
but I drop whatever it was I was reaching for.

I run,
        trip,
                fall
and crack my head and it hurts.
Only then I see a light so bright
there are no more shadows.
        And there it was: the smell and swell
        of it like a sea of glass –
        shining and strange.

I walk down the blurred path,
past rows of houses, all tired and dirty,
inside – the same,
the people – the same.

I'm a ghost amongst kin.
I want to see, to peep
through the curtains, to peel
them open like an onion.

The streets: seagulls and people
moving and breathing, new flats growing
through clouds,
patchwork of green fields and concrete blocks,
Ein cantref, with a hundred languages.

The klaxon of colour: everything you ever needed.
Kebab shops, cornershops,
Taxis, tracksuits,
Clark's Pies, Ice Cream Passion.
Father, mother, child.

Day and Night.

But the world around it slept,
sweet and sound,
and we never thought it would be us.

Then the waves kept hitting and hitting
and we woke to find our streets a black sea.
And now here it is:
Pictures in an old book,
A name on an old map.
A city gone.

Rich Teas

Gaynor ordered Victoria Sponge and milky coffee, which didn't surprise Nathan.

'I'll bring it over when it's ready,' Nathan smiled.

Gaynor sat by the window and breathed heavily as she slumped in her chair which moaned under her weight. A loose screw rattled on the vinyl flooring and Gaynor turned to face the dust frosted window. She saw an old man with a white beard crossing the street. His kuma a crown, the gold and green embroidery flashing in the morning sun. He barely made it to the other side before the lights turned green and the traffic started to flow. He walked past a young man, topless and decorated in ink, shouting hopelessly outside Tesco, without taking any notice. A polyester box flapped in the drain whilst seagulls eyed the overflowing bins. These sights and sounds were an ugly loveliness to Gaynor.

Nathan appeared with the coffee and cake.

'What would I do without you, love?'

'What would we do without you, Gaynor?'

Gaynor turned her head slowly to look across the street.

'"Coffee bar and workspace." Why can't they just call it a café? Who sells coffee for more than £2.50 around 'ere? I've 'eard they 'aven't even plastered the walls. And guess what they 'ave there on a Saturday morning?'

'What?'

'Well guess, you 'ave to guess, that's the game.'

Nathan knew, but to humour Gaynor, he said, 'Life drawing classes?'

'Eh? 'Eck no! Worse if you ask me – Yoga classes! In a café! All that sweat and lycra and then people are supposed to enjoy their coffee and cake there! Grangetown is changing I'm telling you! And they don't accept cash! Jesus!'

Nathan flinched.

'Sorry, love. Didn't think. Will you sit down with me?'

He sat opposite Gaynor and studied her as she cut a slice of the cake. It was hard to tell how old Gaynor was. Deep wrinkles, the odd long whisker on her chin, salt and pepper hair and the odour of talc. She kept repeating the same stories: where her grandchildren were at; how she lodged with a Welsh speaking Presbyterian minister when she was eighteen; how her grandmother would say *cwtch* for cuddle; how everybody thought her Uncle Ned from Pwllheli was batshit crazy, but he wasn't, it was just that he only spoke Welsh. But people did look older than their real age here. Take the 9C bus a mile to the north to Pontcanna and forty-year-olds look half their age, their jeans tight and foreheads frozen.

'Tell me Nathan, 'ow's your mother?'

Gaynor used to attend the same church as Nathan; a small house church that met at his parent's house. Nathan remembers sitting on his father's lap when he was younger, his father stroking his hair slowly. He explained that there were Sheep and Goats in the world. And that the Sheep were the Elect and that the Goats were everyone else, including the kind people in the church on the roundabout at the bottom of Corporation Road and that only the Sheep, that is the Elect, would go to Heaven and see Jesus. Nathan had a nightmare that night. He dreamt that he was in a dark place so that there was no floor, nor ceiling, nor walls. Just darkness with a monstrous goat chasing him. He woke up sweating and crying and his father ran into his bedroom and prayed with him, but all Nathan wanted was a cwtch from his mother, and Nathan nearly vomited because his father's pyjamas smelled of dried goat skin.

'Oh, she's fine thank you,' Nathan answered. Gaynor raised her eyebrows.

One day, whilst reading C. S. Lewis in the living room, Nathan heard a crash from the kitchen. When he opened the door, he saw Bolognese in a heap on the dark tiled floor and a white plate smashed into trillions of tiny pieces. His mother was holding her face with a trembling hand and his father stood by her, right fist clenched and a vein pulsating on his temple. All the make up in the world couldn't cover the bruise, and the following Sunday Nathan remembered Gaynor speaking with his mother in whispers. Gaynor never went to their church again.

'Good. Remember me to her, will you? Such a pretty woman. How about you Nathan? Still single?'

*

The first time Nathan saw Sadia was at Clare's café. Nathan was reading the menu for the billionth time when the door opened. Nathan noticed the black Vans Old Skools, then white drainpipe jeans followed by the loose Nike hoody and the pink hijab and then dark brown eyes that were the most intense sugar rush. She wore mis-matched neon green and pink socks and carried a red penny board and ordered a black Americano. She smiled when Nathan gave her the change and their hands touched.

'I'll bring it over when it's ready,' Nathan managed to say.

He watched her as she made her way across the café and

when she was sitting down, she reached into her rucksack and took out a large book.

'What's the book?' Nathan asked after placing the Americano down, with a great deal of the drink now in the saucer because of his shaking hands.

'*Blankets*. It's a comic, but it's really serious.'

'Oh. I've never read comics.'

'Never?'

'No. I like C.S. Lewis though. I've read the Welsh translations too.'

'Cool. *Diolch* for the coffee.'

'Thanks. *Croeso!*'

'What?'

'You're welcome.'

'Oh! Cool. *Croeso*. I'll remember that.'

'What's your name?'

'Sadia.'

'Nathan.'

'Nice to meet you, Nathan.'

Sadia returned the following week carrying her penny board and wearing mis-matched stripy socks this time.

'Hi Nathan!' He noticed that she had dimples when she smiled. And she was smiling. At him.

'Hi, Sadia. What can I get for you?'

'I'm not stopping, sorry, but I want you to have this.'

Sadia took *Blankets* out of her bag and slid it across the counter. 'It's epic. I'm not sure how it compares to C. S. Lewis. I've never read his stuff, but I'm sure you'll like this.'

'Thanks… but I can't.' Nathan felt hot and fuzzy. He had Googled the book after their conversation and deleted his search history in panic after reading the synopsis on the internet.

'My parents…they're quite strict,' he summarised.

'Jehovah's?'

'No.'

'Salvation Army?'

'Nope.'

'Mormon!'

'No.'

'What then?'

Nathan hesitated. 'Erm… The Elect.'

'The what?'

'Hmmm, they're just different from your average church goer. Like, Brexit is prophesied in the Bible, and Trump is a good guy different.'

'Oh. The Elect. Sounds like a lame indie band!'

They both laughed. Nathan liked the fact that they were laughing, together.

'Yeah. Well, that's us. I'm on bass and my father's the lead singer.'

'Of course, you're on bass.'

'Why?'

'All the cute ones play bass.'

Nathan wanted to beat his chest and roar and dance and shout hallelujah.

'Well, Nathan, my 'rents are sort of tapped as well.' He liked the way she said his name, as if she had been saying it for years in her sleep, in the shower, in the kitchen, whilst lying on the sofa and when out in the park, and that she enjoyed saying it. 'Why do you think I came here last week? No offence like but it wasn't for the coffee. I wouldn't let my parents see me reading this, so I go around cafés to read. Get me?'

'Sure.' Then Nathan had a brainwave. 'What are you doing Saturday afternoon?' He couldn't believe that he was saying those words.

'Saturday afternoon I'm at the skate park with Nadia... I can't ditch Nadia. But I could meet you after? Around 6pm? What did you have planned?'

*

Kaspas was packed. The cheap leather seats squeaked as knees and hands and dirty shoes climbed all over them. Glitter sparkled in the walls and orders were screamed in a frenzy. Sadia and Nathan sat in the furthest corner from the door. They closed the book when their pancakes arrived.

'That was dark. Did that really happen?' Nathan asked.

'Yeah. It's auto-biographical.'

'Wow.'

'It's good isn't it?'

'It's powerful.'

'It's real.'

They pulled the plate of pancakes and vanilla ice cream towards them.

'Have you ever tried *roti*?' Sadia asked.

'What?'

'*Roti*. Of course, you haven't. It's a sort of flatbread.' Sadia grabbed a pancake in her hand and scooped up the ice cream with it. Nathan was holding his spoon in his hand. 'With *roti* the idea is you scoop up rice or vegetables with it. Like this...'

She held the pancake high, now with ice cream pouring down her hand, dripping all over the table. They were both laughing and smiling vanilla ice cream smiles.

They met every Saturday until they finished the book and each week they read more slowly, not wanting their meetings at Coffi Co., Little Man Coffee and as far east as Early Bird to end. They feasted on custard filled doughnuts and velvety Flat Whites. They complained about their parents and discussed election forecast polls and Nathan wished that the hands on his Timex watch would slow the heck down.

'Hello, Nathan.'

It was Keith who saw them. Keith was from church. They were leaving Blue Honey on City Road and Sadia had just set off on her penny board. Nathan was still drunk from the smell of her perfume and roasted veg. Keith had obviously seen them saying good bye to each other, their cwtch lasting that second longer than a cwtch between just friends ought to; their cheeks brushing against each other.

'Hi Keith.' Nathan looked down at his new red Vans Old Skools.

'A Muslim?'

News spread fast along the Elect network. His father was sitting on the sofa in the living room. Nathan only remembers his father giving him a cwtch once, and it was on that sofa. He was ten and it was stuffy. His father lifted his arm and told Nathan to cwtch up as they were watching a nature programme. They cwtched and sweated as they watched a male lion maul and eat a cub that wasn't his.

'How did you meet her? How long has this been going on? Are you sleeping with her? Have you converted? God have mercy. Do you know how this looks? Selfish, selfish boy. This could be the end of my church.'

His father ordered him to

'SIT DOWN'

at the kitchen table and think what

'PAIN

And

DISTRESS'

he had caused his mother.

'At least I don't hit Mother!' Nathan stood, pushed his way past his father towards the door.

His father grabbed him and swung him around and struck him. Nathan heard a crack and felt a gush of blood streaming hot from his nose.

It was dark, and the rain tickled Nathan. He ran down Pentrebane Street towards the boarded up Con Club. The shutters of Grange Fish Bar were being drawn shut. His feet drummed the pavement, waking the neighbourhood's dogs. Barks and wails woke the night as if the dogs could smell the blood that was still pouring from Nathan's nose. He turned right into Grange Gardens. Bats dived above his head. Insects scurried under the cover of leaves. He smelt the sickly scent of weed and heard giggling coming from the bandstand.

He found himself standing outside Sadia's house with his heart pounding and mouth and chin caked in blood. When he stormed out of his parents' house he wasn't sure what his plan was, but here he was, his arm slowly rising and watching in horror as his hand knocked the door. He heard soft feet on wooden floor and then the door opened and through a gap between the green door and the frame, he saw Sadia's perfect face.

'Nathan. What are you doing here?' She opened the door a little wider. The strange smell of harissa made Nathan think of God and Heaven and everything good. 'You're bleeding! What happened?'

For the first time she held his face in her hands and used her thumb to wipe away the blood.

Nathan closed his eyes and even though his nose was broken he felt lovely. He opened his eyes to pull Sadia towards him but stopped himself from doing so. He tasted the blood in his mouth. All he wanted was a cwtch.

'I'm sorry,' Nathan said, and ran.

As Nathan stepped back into the warmth of his parents' kitchen he felt ten years old again.

His parents were sitting at the dinner table with steaming mugs of tea and a plate of untouched Rich Teas on the table in front of them. It was his mother who used to take him to his piano exams. The exams took place in an old chapel. They would sit quietly in the freezing waiting room, Nathan warming his hands above an electric radiator and his mother tapping her legs nervously. Five minutes before his exam was due his mother would give him a Rich Tea. When his name was called she would give him a cwtch and squeeze every inch of breath out of him and only then Nathan would know that everything would be ok and if he only stuck to what he had practised and what he had learned and not veer from what he knew he would pass the exam and his mother would be proud and his father pleased.

Nathan looked at his parents sitting at the table. He felt claustrophobic but glad to be home. He wanted to scream and shout but all he did was go to the table and reach for a Rich Tea. He recited the mantra in his head. Stick to what you know. Don't go off track. Don't veer off the narrow path. Practice what's been taught to you. Make Mother proud. Please Father. He might not eat you alive after all. He shut the door behind him and was cwtched by his mother, every hope squeezed out of him. His father went to boil the kettle.

*

Nathan locked the till and turned off the radio. He zig-zagged passed the plastic chairs and peeling tables and turned off the lights before opening the door. He fought with the stiff lock but inevitably heard it slot into place. The sun had started to set and Grangetown was glorious and still, like the second between the dazzle of a firework and the bang. Nathan walked home down the Taff Trail. The evening air was sharp and the smell of the hops from Brains was thick. Two men were fishing under the bridge. Their rods were still. The university rowing team were heading upriver, overtaking the river taxi where tourists sipped wine and zoomed their lenses. Streams of cyclists made their way home in both directions and Nathan could hear the rolling sound of a penny board growing louder and louder behind him.

Jon Doyle

Hardly Dead

Annie woke one morning to find she had no pulse. She tried her wrist, her neck, her temple. She tried behind the knee. But nothing. A meaty stillness.

Against her better judgement, she typed the question into Google. *What does it mean when you have no pulse?*

Reading the top few links, she dragged herself to the bathroom mirror. She didn't look especially dead, nor did she feel it, but maybe that's what all corpses thought. Turning her head this way and that, she assessed herself from various angles. She took off her top and examined her shoulders and chest. A little pale perhaps, a little too veiny, but hardly dead.

To call in sick would be to dwell on the issue so she prepared for work. The major question of Annie's morning schedule was whether to shower or eat breakfast. Doing both felt like a luxury she couldn't afford, and making a decision so early in the morning proved bracing. Breakfast didn't appeal—Google had warned low appetite to be a symptom of those with no pulse—so she undressed and stood in the shower but no matter how she turned the tap the water ran cold.

*

Annie couldn't concentrate. Pamela said she looked terrible and she laughed in her face. 'What did you expect?' Annie asked. Pamela didn't have an answer. What *did* Pamela expect?

Perfection?

The phone rang and Annie answered it, parroting the welcome lines she was expected to parrot in the voice with which she'd been taught to parrot them. She had a framed picture of a dog on her desk and she studied it as she spoke. It was a random dog. She'd printed it from the internet.

'I think I've got the wrong number,' the caller said, putting down the phone. Annie kept the line open, the dial tone ringing like struck glass.

Pamela was punching holes in stacks of documents. Annie watched as the small circles snowed across her keyboard and desk, sticking to the damp warmth of Pamela's palms. Sensing she had an audience, Pamela looked up and flashed a smile. A complicated smile, equal parts pity and encouragement and straight up concern. A mother's smile, if you will.

Annie didn't dislike Pamela, or anyone with whom she worked, but resented something about their characters, the way they refused to let her slip through their attention.

'Hey, Pam,' she called. 'Have you heard back from Nick?'

Pamela furrowed her brow and looked at Annie over her glasses, as though trying to gauge whether she was joking. Playful disappointment was a habit of hers, doubling up as a kind of vigilance against any mockery that went over her head.

'Which email did I miss?'

'We're meeting in fifteen minutes,' Pamela revealed. 'All of us. You were supposed to —'

Annie raised a finger toward her colleague. 'Let me grab a pen,' she said into the phone, pretending the call was live

114

and urgent. 'Uh huh, uh huh.' She swirled the pen across a series of post-it notes like a drunk celebrity at Comic-Con.

The dial tone purred in her ear, the texture of warm oil.

*

They met in their soon-to-be office, an open plan space with no computer monitors or telephone lines. Private offices encouraged an atmosphere of distrust and ill-feeling, the memo had said. Seating plans bred a false sense of security. They'd be hot desking from the following week onwards.

'We're looking to set up an environment of wellbeing and motivation,' Nick explained to those gathered before him. 'We aim to facilitate the natural transmission of ideas.'

Annie's limbs felt heavy. Taking two fingers, she traced her wrist as casually as possible, as though nonchalance was a barrier against whatever was happening. She felt bone, tendon, but no pulse.

'I appreciate that,' Tammy said, 'but the pilot day raised some concerns.'

Nick nodded, holding a smile. Tammy had been elected as the unofficial spokesperson. She could maintain eye contact through considerable discomfort. They had every faith in her abilities.

'I'm going to level with you,' Nick said, lowering his voice and glancing at the door. Nick was always levelling with them. It was a part of his job. Nick was paid to be sympathetic, a stepping stone between the workers and the bosses. To listen but not act. To listen and forget. 'Personally, I see the issues with open plan designs. I work in the office myself.'

'With all due respect,' Tammy replied, 'if you truly saw the issues you wouldn't have greenlighted the plan after the trial.'

Murmurs of approval. Annie ran her fingers over her neck. She'd considered calling the doctor but was afraid of the crash cart and compressions. She'd read once that they break your ribs.

'The office got so noisy that you couldn't take a simple phone call,' Tammy was saying. 'My staff took work home in order to concentrate after hours.'

A faint tapping in the distance. The entire room fell silent, listening to its unhurried approach. Nick swallowed and hitched his trousers and reapplied his smile. Leslie J. Nelson, the company's CEO, wore expensive shoes that sounded like high-heels. Their clop echoed through the fashionably minimal corridors.

The doors opened and Nelson emerged. He was a small man with protruding teeth and a bald head, taken to walking around with his eyebrows raised as if the entire world came as an unpleasant surprise. The expression gave him a shark-like quality—not a mighty Great White but something smaller, a lesser species that hangs around coral reefs, gets dragged dead from the ocean in the nets of trawlers.

'Mr. Nelson,' Nick said, 'we were just discussing the new environment.'

'And?'

'And we have some concerns,' Tammy said.

Nelson looked past Tammy at the rest of his staff. 'Is that right? We?'

No-one said a word. For the first time Tammy glanced over her shoulder.

'The new environment...' Nelson began, off walking again. 'The new environment was not plucked from thin air.'

His shoes clacked one way, stopped, clacked back. Annie pinched herself, bit her cheek. She scrunched her eyes and covered her ears and tried to focus on the blood inside her head. But there was nothing there.

'Intensive research was conducted,' Nelson said, 'by experts in the field.' He stopped his pacing and took a step toward Tammy. 'But you... we, have some concerns?'

Tammy swallowed. 'Mr Nelson, it was my understanding that the purpose of the trial was to elicit feedback so as to improve the new system, to iron out any kinks before we make the switch. In the days after the test, several members of my staff confided that they were forced to take home the work that required the most focus and concentration due to the conditions in the office.'

'In the environment,' Nick said.

Nelson laughed like beached fish. He tried to speak through gulps of air.

Perhaps I am dead, Annie thought. Perhaps that's not the worst thing? You've nothing to lose when you're dead. You can take pleasure in melancholy and spite. Annie watched Nelson guffawing before her, white spittle collecting at the corners of his mouth. She imagined placing her hands around his neck, her fingers lacing behind his ears and pushing her palms against his throat. She imagined the machinery there, the nerves and tubing, the muscular reflexes as her grip tightened. Nelson's eyes would widen as the oxygen ceased, his brows forced over the top of his skull. She imagined the thrumming life beneath her palms, wondering if it was hers or his as the tick of blood tapered off within her grip.

' — an uncomfortable temperature when the windows are closed,' Tammy was explaining, 'but with them open the ambient noise far exceeds an acceptable — '

'Nick,' Nelson barked, 'the window, please. Let's hear this so-called unacceptable ambient noise.'

Moving with the skittering need to please that school bullies had tried and failed to eradicate throughout his childhood, Nick approached the window. He removed the latch and pushed the pane. No sooner had it opened did some hurtling force descend upon them, a meteoric flash of panic and movement.

The gathered workers pushed apart, a directionless action of self-preservation.

'Gaaaaaahhh!' Nelson screamed, raising his hands to protect his head.

Only Annie stayed where she was, fingers still probing for an absent carotid throb. Before her landed a small bird, purple and green but with the beak of a raven, like starling and crow collided. It stopped and stared with gravid stillness, the hunted inaction of hellhounds and house spiders. It was looking straight at Annie.

'Someone get it,' Nelson yelled, crouching low against a desk 'Someone catch the thing!'

Annie's position as the only person standing was an act of involuntary volunteering, though she didn't argue. The bird was here for her and her it was going to get.

She'd seen this stuff on TV. One step, then another. Avoid sudden movements. Be wary of the head. She walked with her arms extended, palms raised. An unarmed carjacker. A priest in benediction. 'It's okay,' she said aloud. 'It's okay.'

The bird held its nerve, eyeing her, a coiled spring.

With each step, Annie brought her hands in. Shoulder width, head width, the width of her neck. As she reached the bird she brought her hands together, palms out and thumbs crossed to form a solid catcher's mitt.

As though reacting to the movement, the bird grew agitated, head flicking this way and that. Its wings unfolded, feathers all askew, and next thing Annie knew the shape hit her in the chest, knocking her backwards not through force but surprise.

Annie sat up and the room gawked. Her hands were clutched at her chest, held tight against a manic motion within. The bird thrashed its head, pushed its wings against its prison, but Annie kept her hands closed. There was something special about the movement in her grip, so small and delirious. She wanted to share it with the others. Come see, she'd call. Come feel him kick.

Before she could speak there was a subtle change in the movement, some ebb at its centre that caused her heart to sink. The flapping became a fluttering, the fluttering not much of anything at all. Already, Annie thought. You've only just begun.

The bird might have been exhausted or merely a realist, like a fish on a line coming to understand its predicament, finding calm in the release. Some things are bigger than you, the bird was saying. To deny this is to betray yourself. The thought incensed Annie. It boiled her blood. Who was this bird to give up so easily? With her, no less, her without pulse. Because she knew. There was no calm in surrender. There was only violence. What if she was to mash her palms, tighten her grip, slowly, slowly, crush inwards until the blood and feathers and bright-black beak were oozing through her fingers? What then?

Annie looked up and the found the others looking back. Pamela looked terrified, she noticed, but still offered a sad, hopeful smile. An instinct, an unconscious thing. A real knockout smile. Feathers tickled Annie's palms and she found herself smiling back.

Getting to her feet, Annie made her way toward the window, hands held aloft. The others followed, forming a procession. Concern and relief bound tight. They saw themselves in the windows, reflected in the glass.

Annie got to the opening and used the clutched ball of her hands to make it wider. She rested her arms on the ledge as traffic traversed the street below. The sun was out, she noticed. The day was passing by. Something about the light and the noise and the gentle lilting breeze changed the situation. Something about the crowd gathered to watch. The bird's acquiescence had taken on a new meaning. What if it wasn't surrender but hope? What if life slid in that direction, and only struggle nudged it off course?

There was a beat in her grasp now, a strong, rhythmic pulse, and she wondered if it was the bird's heart or her own.

The scene played in slow motion as she released her grip, fists unfurling around a ball of feathers. She offered the bird the open air, a place of its own. She flicked her palms up to launch the creature skyward. The breeze seemed to stir the bird, remind it of its position on this earth, and it opened its wings in tandem and made to fly but did not—some catch or miscue skewing the action. It tilted to the left and, with one last shudder of wing, plunged downward.

Jannat Ahmed

Essence

I could do without another #poem word –
our *staccato* and *petrichor* swamp,
a leech-y *bleeding on to the page*,

silences

all *brokens*, all *hearts*,
all *in loves* and *true loves* –
wrangled into black,
on white paper and white screens,
as if we are one being, writing
an endless series of bodies
verb-ing some *something*
always *always* in the nude

sometimes –
too often –
traumatised
at the hand or eye or hips
of a patriarch

and, of course, a woman
claiming herself in the night
or daylight
or limelight

a shared fantasy of the commune,
coming into being
       legato-like
          pouring
              s
                m
                 o
                  o
                 t
              h
                  into ready *cups you'll bring to your lips*

pungent with *desire* to bend, break, blow, burn a language new
unscented with the body
of work and millennia

Poets' *tongues* and throats and lungs
who undo
redo, undo
strikethrough
word after
pause

~~after~~
line-break
after clause,
cook in the heat *of their mouths*
the subtle-strongest words they know

until *crisp*
and *golden*

white space
arranged on a printing plate just so

at the writer's neck, lobe, wrist (*come close, come close*)
inhale
a custom scent of their own –
eau de poésie, de parle, de mots[1]*:
essence of poets read and poems known,
ten thousand times a sense than taste alone.

---

[1] *A play on eau de parfum. Water of poetry, speech, words*

December White

December White sounds like the colour of paint:
a pot chosen for the sake of nostalgia,
rather than the silver sheen you notice
days later in the twilight of a blue velvet lamp.

Sophie Evans

Losing Touch

I tried to lie still but my back kept springing into an arch. A nurse held my hand whilst the doctor inserted a long needle into my spine. Once in, he pushed it further into my back so it was tightly secured within the skin. A nurse patted my forehead with a damp cloth, about as useful as a plaster may have been to stop the blood that drenched the sheets I lay on. They had told me in the ante-natal classes that at this point my cervix should be almost ten centimetres dilated but mine had let me down. It had stretched to only half of that and so with every push the skin became thinner and raw.

'One last push now, lovely.'

Then, a loud call of my name came from the hallway. A moment later Mum crashed into the room, balloons caught in the doorframe. She sat beside me and told me it would be ok and I believed her even when I felt the flesh of my body tear and blood gush down my swollen thighs as the head forced through. The pressure between my legs pushed further. Then, my body fell back, empty, onto the pillow and a few moments later a nurse handed him over to me. He needed me. He cried until I held him close against my chest to feed whilst the doctor stitched up the wound further down the bed. That was the very first time I held my son.

'Excuse me, are you getting on today?'

I jolted, looking up to see the driver of the 49 bus staring down at me again, twisting his lips.

'I'm just waiting for the rain to stop,' I threw at him quickly, before realising it was no longer raining. How embarrassing. I had dozed off into another daydream of the past again. It happened frequently. He sighed and the doors hissed shut. I looked back over at the lady beside me. She sat there on the pale red bench of the shelter with surprising elegance, smugly holding her rounded tummy. A gust of wind blew through the gap of the shelter, ruffling the tops of our head but the hank of her ponytail remained unmoved. Next to her, a little girl with matching copper hair neatly weaved into a french plait. Both had freckled, porcelain skin.

'What about Isabella?' asked the little girl, whilst leaning her head gently onto her mother's bump. Then they both quickly turned to look at one another in delight. 'She likes it Mummy! She likes it!'

'Yes darling, she does. Let's hope it's definitely a little girl then.' As she said it, she looked over at me with a large smirk, inviting me into their private happiness. 'We've got one boy at home already you see, what a handful!' She spoke with a voice that was warm and crinkly.

'Yes they are aren't they,' I replied.

'Do you have any?' I had been asked this question many times, and my answer was well rehearsed.

'Yes. One boy. Four. Cheeky little fella but boys will be boys won't they,' I replied mechanically.

She grinned back. 'Oh definitely. Poor Lucy here is desperate for a sister.' I smiled back at her and then at Lucy who was preoccupied by the oncoming bus.

'Is this ours, Mummy?'

'Yes, darling.'

Sam and I used to go on our little adventures, starting

from this very spot. He would sit so well behaved, if a little noisy, on my lap whilst we waited. No trouble at all. We'd guess what colour car would be next to pass us but if it turned left before the bus stop, you didn't win the point. He always guessed red, that being his favourite colour. There never seemed to be very many red cars so I always guessed ridiculous colours like purple or yellow and just once, a yellow Corsa came up over the brow and we both sat there, mouths and eyes open wide. Of course it turned at the junction, resulting in us standing there, bent over in laughter.

'No points for you, Mummy!' he managed to squeeze in, between fits of mischievous giggles.

There is something quite alarming about recalling a warm memory, and feeling frozen numb. I had not been called Mummy in four years. We were inseperable. Me and my son, Sam. My son Sam. I said it so often, so easily with speed that it became a new collection of words: Myson Sam. For a long time I missed it. It felt like waking up, shivering cold in the middle of the night with no warm blanket to drag over your head. Recently though, I barely felt it was even a part of me. Still, when someone asked if I had children, how could I ever say no? You see, when a wife loses their husband they become a widow. It's not easy but it is simple. The mother of a dead child has no title to explain herself to others and it only gets more complicated for someone like me, the mother of a missing child.

My pocket buzzed. Two texts, three missed calls.

"Hope you're ok hun. Let me know if you want to come over Sunday. I'm cooking roast beef. Love you, Mum xx"

She never understood that I knew it was her because I'd saved her number. She always felt the need to sign a text. The next message just told me that I had two new voicemail messages. I listened to both, one of which was, of course,

127

Mum repeating what she had said in the text but the other was a local journalist requesting an interview. She said, she 'thought it would be a good way to commemorate five years since Sam had gone missing, and give the public a freshen up of the facts so they are reminded to keep a look out for this poor little boy.'

If I had enough in my bank account to replace it, I would have thrown the phone across the road. Two years ago I sat at home begging every newspaper to print the story once more in hope of bringing light to the investigation. Hope had disintegrated with each passing day since it had happened, but now I didn't live in hope. I survived. That was all.

I looked at my watch. 2:25. Five more minutes and the 49 bus would be returning. I pulled my jeans unstuck from the bench, took my first real breath of the day, and began walking towards Cromwell Street. It was quite a posh area. The sort of place you imagine yourself at thirty-five, maybe forty, with a couple of children, a husband and a golden retriever. Each of the houses were unique, like a patchwork quilt, but all had an air of wealth. My favourite was a large champagne stone cottage that stood in a garden of rose bushes. The lawn was far greener than real grass and neatly trimmed to frame the path that led up towards an extravagant, brass handled door. Further along, I could hear a frantic cry of a middle aged woman. 'James stop it. Stop it right now!'

I crossed the road in order to follow the noise that led me to the driveway of a large red brick house. In front of it a small boy carrying a hose pipe and a Cheshire cat smile ran dodging his mother who repeatedly lunged at him, only to get sprayed again. I hurried past, amused.

I took a left at the corner shop where the smell of fresh bread oozed out of the door temptingly, and then the second left at the garage before carrying on down to Thomas town. I needed to sit. I rubbed the spots of sweat on my palms into my jeans. My coat hid the dark patch on the back of my shirt thankfully. I carried on for a couple of minutes more until I reached the bench directly opposite the park. I did whatever I could to avoid looking over. Since losing Sam, schools, playgrounds, any family orientated places had become hard to be around. I replied to Mum, "*sounds lovely Mum, get to yours for 12? xx.*"

I looked at Facebook momentarily. It's Jane Seagull, and five other friends' birthday today. Want to help them celebrate? No thank you.

Another text from Mum. "*Perfect. How are you feeling today? Love you, Mum xx.*" I always hated answering that question. It felt like a bad thing, lying to Mum.

"*Not too bad, hope you're well xx,*" I replied. She knew I was lying. She asked me so often, she had become well accustomed to the reel of possible responses including: 'Not too bad', 'Up and down' and 'Could be better', all translating to 'absolutely shit'.

She didn't reply. It was nearly three o'clock so I knew she'd be on her way to pick up my nephews.

Over the road children screeched and laughed as they whirled swiftly on the roundabout. I glanced over, unable to distract myself any longer. There were four children in the park. A pair of twin girls sporting identical pink coats were being pushed on the swings. The one little girl begged her dad to go 'higher, higher' whilst the other gritted her teeth and silently clung to the chains either side of her. The vibrant colours that once decorated the climbing frame when I took Sam here, had turned to a pale blush and powder blue. A little boy, perhaps three or four, carefully made his way back down after his mother insisted him do so. She waited there with open arms anxiously for the moment she could reach her son and bring him into her safely. He had beautiful dark brown eyes and a mop of black curls.

Nothing like my fair Sam but he reminded me of him. He looked at his mother with a warmth and love like Sam had looked at me.

It took me back again. I thought of how I had stood where she stood, clapping, congratulating Sam on getting all the way across. Was I too careless? After that, Sam had felt hungry so we sat together on the grass, and ate cheese sandwiches and shared a chocolate eclair. He wanted to play hide and seek so we did. I counted first, covering my eyes, leaving small gaps between my fingers to see where he was headed. I saw him run over to a group of trees nearby. He crouched to the floor and sat there in a ball excitedly, waiting for me to count down. I then covered my eyes fully to avoid him calling me a cheat and counted down the remaining seconds. Sixteen seconds. That was all it took for him to disappear. I wandered around pretending to guess where he could be and then once I thought it seemed realistic enough, I made my way over to where he had hidden himself.

Sam was no longer there. Sam was gone. He was far more clever than most five-year-old boys so I assumed he had tricked me. Perhaps he knew I would watch him and waited for me to stop so he could find another hiding place. After a couple of minutes, I began to feel the worry a parent practically bathes in twice a month. It's that worry you feel in the supermarket when you walk down the central aisle and turn your head quickly, left, to right, to left and so on, checking every other aisle for your child, or when they run ahead of you towards a busy road. I circled the large oak where I'd seen him several times and scoured the branches above. There was a row of trees that looked similar each side of that one, so I checked those next. Nothing. Behind them lay a large rugby field and further again, a much larger forest. He knew he couldn't go beyond the trees, surely he would not test that rule. Ten minutes later, I found myself angry at him. I shouted his name with a rage, preserving my nerves by convincing myself that he was playing a trick on me. Now, sometimes I wonder if he'd heard me shout, perhaps I scared him off.

A young teenage girl walking a large German Shepherd had joined me in the playground. I asked her to help me find my son and we searched for another ten minutes or so. Then she looked at me, eyebrows tilted, more than just concerned. She told me I should ring the police. One hour later I was questioned for a detailed account of the incident in the local police station. Two days later I stood in front of the press, appealing for any evidence or eye witnesses to help the case of my missing son. A month later I had to leave my job as a primary school teacher. A year later the case ran cold, and four years and two months on, today, I sat watching a mother with her son in the same park I lost mine.

I wondered if they noticed me watching them. Soon the woman picked up her handbag, swung it over her shoulder and held her son's hand the entire short journey back to the car. When I looked back towards the playground my attention was drawn to another child there, sitting in the overgrown grass, untangling a kite. My body fell silent but for the shudder that rippled down my spine. He had fine, ash blond hair that curled at the ends and a nose just like my mum's, wide and flat. His ears poked out slightly, his shoulders were wide, and his lips puckered naturally. It couldn't be. But it must be, I thought. Sam. It was Sam.

My cheeks quickly became wet with tears sinking into my pores as I stared at him and every detail that had grown in the last four years. That would make him nine. I had a nine year old. I had never been so delighted to feel my age.

I rose from the bench, legs taut. I took a long, closer look. Not Sam. Winded by what felt like a second loss of my son, the bench caught me with its sturdy frame. I sat. I cried. I asked Sam, where are you? I asked God, where is he? Then, with no real reason or explanation I felt myself change. In one single moment, my head was clear, unbound by the strands of chaos that had knotted within for so long. In that moment I knew he was truly gone and I could no longer find him.

Rhea Seren Phillips

MaE ALCemI Rhyfedd yn EiN ClymuA PECuliAR AlcheMy TiEs uS

Anomalistic argot; catalyse
gabble as homogenised shrieks.
Anglicise gas leaks; rupture squeaks,
alluviums that abscise
for nationalised rebellion, chastise
grief as womb oxidise,   reekiss.
Troubled youth piques haggard techniques;
Wren cusps its beak; she shakes the sky.

Silhouettes swear strange despair.
Beware of this wandering art;
lingua franca im.part
azure dart of cold solitaire;
they seek to ensnare anywhere
but mid-air where   they dare   to   dart.
It's all a smart   te   a   ring apart
of the appraised zealot chair.

Acknowledgements

This year has been a difficult year as a result of Covid Nineteen. The dedication of trustees and volunteers is ongoing, technology has replaced "live" meetings.

Trustees are: Phil Knight, Chairman; Amanda O'Neil, Secretary; Liza Osborne; Kirsty Parsons; Huw Pudner, and past prize-winners Rose Widlake, Jonathan Edwards, Glyn Edwards, and Natalie Holborow.
Volunteers: Michael O'Neil, Brendan and Kym Barker, Bob Thomas, Donna Lewis, Nathan Davies and Katie Rees.

Malcolm Lloyd provides the most comprehensive web-site. It details all the past prize winners, details about the award, videos of past prize-winning presentation evenings, poems and pints evenings, as well as poems at Victoria Gardens Neath.

Thank you to Neath Port Talbot Borough Council. Thank you to Neath Town Council for an annual grant aid. As well as for the hire of Neath Old Town Hall for the Presentation Evening. Individual donations come from past prize-winner Chistopher Hyatt, Jen and Mike Wilson, Margot Morgan, Dave and Gwyneth Hughes, Byron and Sandra Beynon, Patrick Dobbs, Ioan and Iris Richard. Liz Hobbs and Steve Croke, Linda Kinsey, Margaret Webley.

Books donated towards fund-raising come from Parthian Books (Richard Lewis Davies). Thanks as well to Carly Holmes from Parthian who is involved in the production of *Cheval 13*. Books also donated from Sally Jones.

Thank you to the editors of *Cheval 13*, Natalie Holborow and Molly Holborn. Past *Cheval* books have been edited by Jonathan Edwards, Glyn Edwards and Rose Widlake; all are previous prize-winners.

Our main source of funding comes from Cheval Neath Poems and Pints. Recordings of the evenings can be found on the website: www.chevalwriters.org.uk (go to heading 'Events'). Thank you to Malcolm Lloyd for the website and to Michael O'Neill for filming. Thanks to photographers Nathan Davies and Katie Rees.

Thank you for donations for raffle prizes at Cheval Neath Poems and Pints, as well as for the hamper donations at the Awards Evening and for administration of the raffle, Liza Osborne and Donna Lewis.

Thank you for the ongoing support of past prize-winners by attending Awards Evenings and messages on social media: Jonathan Edwards, Glyn Edwards, Anna Lewis, Siôn Tomos Owen, Joao Morais, Eluned Gramich, Mari Ellis, Rhian Elizabeth, Rhys Owain Williams, Carl Griffin, Liz Wride, Robin Ganderton, Emily Blewitt, Cynan Llwyd, Catrin Lawrence, Whyt Pugh, Gareth Smith, Mao Oliver Semenov, Georgia Carys Williams, Emily Hancox, Thomas Tyrrell, Christina Thatcher.

We are most grateful to Neath Port Talbot Community Voluntary Services for their support and registration as a voluntary organisation.

Author Biographies

Jannat Ahmed was born and grew up in Barry, Wales and is co-founder and editor-in-chief at *Lucent Dreaming*, independent magazine for writing and art. She graduated with a master's degree in English Literature from Cardiff University and is better known as Subscriptions and Marketing Officer at *Poetry Wales* where she introduced, and now manages, Wales Poetry Award, Wales Young Poets Award/Gwobr Beirdd Ifanc Cymru and Wales Poetry Day. She has previously performed at Where I'm Coming From as a featured artist, and has appeared at Seren Cardiff Poetry Festival with *Lucent Dreaming*.

Megan Charlton has moved to Aberystwyth from Edinburgh, to study alleviating metal mine pollution with plants and bacteria. This piece is her first published piece, however she self publishes poetry on a blog through the pseudonym purplesouppoet. She picked up writing poetry after stopping in adolescence, by writing and performing an angry piece after an intense fling, at an open poem night on the Edinburgh fringe. She then irregularly performed poetry in pubs in Edinburgh – the highlight of which was the random happenstance of a folk band complete with harp walking past at 2 am and performing a set of poems about the magic of the plant world to their accompaniment. Having lived in Burnley, and the edge of the Yorkshire dales, she has an interest in the use of dialect words, class, people, and nature.

Elizabeth Rose Choi mostly writes short stories inspired by one of her favourite pastimes: eavesdropping. Amongst other things, she has been inspired by the Brontë sisters and Agatha Christie to write all things wholesome yet bleak. She was raised in the hills of Snowdonia, and went from scribbling away in the back room of her parents' music shop to completing her Creative Writing MA at Cardiff University. Along with other writers from the MA, she helped set up 'A Zoom of Our Own' – an online group who continue to support and encourage each other in their writing ventures. As we speak, Elizabeth is probably sitting in an armchair with a hot chocolate thinking 'what shall I write next?'.

Cara Cullen is from Pontypridd in south Wales. After studying violin in London and then History at the University of Oxford, Cara returned home to work in St. Fagans National Museum of History. During the past few years Cara has been researching Welsh material culture as well as listening to and collecting oral history. Alongside writing, Cara sings and plays the banjo, performing traditional tunes from the British Isles and America as well as songs she has written in both Welsh and English. Most of her interests have been informed by the landscape and natural environment of Wales and Cara is often outdoors fell-running, walking, or more recently gardening.

Rhodri Diaz grew up in a small village on the border between Swansea and Carmarthenshire, and it was there that his love of stories and storytelling first began. He studied Creative Writing at Swansea University and hopes to one day go back to study a Masters. A proud first-language Welsh speaker, Rhodri enjoys writing stories and characters that are deeply rooted in Welsh culture. His stories have previously appeared in *Cheval 10* and *11*, and he is currently writing his first novel.

In his spare time, Rhodri enjoys wandering around castles, petting dogs and buying more books than he'll ever read.

Jon Doyle is from Port Talbot in South Wales. He has an MA in Creative Writing from Cardiff University, and a PhD from Swansea University. His writing has appeared in *The Rumpus*, *Hobart*, *3:AM Magazine*, *Queen Mob's Teahouse*, *The Coachella Review* and other places, and he runs the arts website Various Small Flames.

Sophie Evans is a Welsh writer who enjoys writing prose and more recently has turned her love of film into a love of scriptwriting which she hopes to explore further. She is currently completing her MA in Creative Writing at Cardiff University alongside finishing her debut novel which was shortlisted for Penguin WriteNow 2020.

Eluned Gramich is a writer and translator. She's lived in Germany and Japan, and is now based in Cardiff. She won the inaugural New Welsh Writing Award in 2015 for her memoir of Hokkaido, *Woman Who Brings the Rain*, which was later shortlisted for the Wales Book of the Year. Recently, she has published a novella on the Welsh language protests as part of *Hometown Tales: Wales* (Orion Books). She's currently completing her creative writing PhD at Aberystwyth and Cardiff University while looking after her eight-month-old daughter.

Emily Hancox has been featured in previous *Cheval* anthologies, and has performed her poetry with the Cheval group on numerous occasions. She's achieved a BA Hons degree in Creative and Professional Writing and currently works as a Senior Gallery Manager at The Waterfront Museum. During lockdown 2020 Emily published her fourth poetry collection, *Research and Write*, a collection based on famous figures from history. She continues to study Archaeology, French and Poetry in her spare time, and hopes to progress her career in Cultural and Museum heritage.

Megan Angharad Hunter is from Penygroes, Dyffryn Nantlle in north Wales and is studying Welsh and Philosophy at Cardiff University. Her first Welsh-language short story was published in the summer edition of *O'r Pedwar Gwynt* in 2019 and this year Y Lolfa is publishing her first novel, *tu ôl i'r awyr*, also in Welsh. Megan also has a passion for music; she enjoys writing songs and plays the flute in Cardiff University's Jass Orchestra. 'Wings' is the first short story that she has written in English.

Cynan Llwyd is an author who lives in Grangetown with his wife Rachel and their son. He has published two novels in Welsh, *Tom* and *Pobl Fel Ni* (both published by Y Lolfa). This is the third time his work features in Cheval, having been published in *Cheval 10* and having been a runner up last year. When he's not writing and reading, he watches football and works for Christian Aid.

Jonathan Macho is nearing the finish line of his MA in Creative Writing in Cardiff, where he's lived all his life. He has various short stories published, including in *Cheval*s 10 and 12, *To Hull and Back* humour anthologies, the debut ebook anthology of Square Wheel Press, and as part of Candy Jar Books' *Lucy Wilson Mysteries* series, who are also releasing his debut novel, *The Serpent's Tongue*, this year. He co-hosts a book review and discussion show, Writers on Reading, with Sophie Buchaillard on Penarth Sounds, and they are both members of the 'A Zoom of Our Own' writers' group.

Nathan Munday originally comes from a small village in Carmarthenshire but he now lives in the heart of Snowdonia looking after Tŷ Mawr Wybrnant, the birthplace of Bible translator and language-saviour William Morgan. He no longer has to escape to the mountains because he lives in their midst. He is married to Jenna who originally comes from the Netherlands, and he is trying to learn Dutch in his spare time. He won the M. Wynn Thomas New Scholars Prize (2016), came second in the New Welsh Writing Awards (2016), and has come runner-up twice in the Terry Hetherington Awards (2019, 2020).

Alexandra O'Leary is a writer and student hailing from Swansea. She is currently studying English Literature and Creative Writing in Swansea University. A passionate writer all her life, Alex is currently working on an extended creative piece for her final year of university, with the plan of moulding it into a fully formed novel by 2021. As a proud Welsh woman, Alex hopes to share the history and beauty of Wales with a worldwide audience.

Morgan Owen is a poet and essayist from Merthyr Tudful. In 2019, he published a pamphlet of poems, *moroedd/dŵr*, which won the inaugural Michael Marks Award for Poetry in a Celtic Language. In the same year he published a volume of poems, *Bedwen ar y lloer*. Both were published with Cyhoeddiadau'r Stamp. He also won the 2019 PEN Cymru/Wales Literature Exchange Translation Challenge for translating poems by the Polish poet Julia Fiedorczuk into Welsh. At the beginning of 2020 he received a Literature Wales Author Scholarship to complete a collection of essays in Welsh centred on the post-industrial landscapes of his upbringing. His work is regularly published in *O'r Pedwar Gwynt*, *Y Stamp*, and *Barddas*.

Rhea Seren Phillips is a PhD student at Swansea University (2016-2020) researching the Welsh metrical tradition in English. She has been published by *The Literary Pocketbook, Poetry Wales, Molly Bloom, Envoi* and *Tears in the Fence,* among others. Rhea is based in Llanelli, Wales.

Gareth Smith lives in Neath and enjoys writing short stories and drama. He is currently completing a PhD in English Literature at Cardiff University which explores class and sexuality in post-war British literature. He has previously been published in the *Cheval* anthologies. His other writing credits include a monologue for the BBC Sesh website and a short play for Sherman Cymru's 40th anniversary. He has also contributed to Wales Arts Review. Twitter: @smitgar27

Rhys Swainston is a Postgraduate student studying Clinical and Mental Health Psychology at Swansea University. He has lived in south Wales his whole life, growing up in Church Village and educated at Ysgol Gyfun Gymraeg Garth Olwg. He is fluent in Welsh. Rhys has a number of small writing achievements to his name. He won an English creative writing competition for his school Eisteddfod. He also worked as the Creative Writing Editor for Swansea University's official magazine, *Waterfront.* His passion for writing gothic horror fiction began when he briefly volunteered as an assistant tour guide at Llancaiach Fawr, famous for being one of the most haunted houses in Britain. Sadly, he did not see any ghosts. As well as horror pieces, Rhys also writes dramatic and comedic stories, as well as science-fiction and fantasy short stories. He has never not wanted to be a writer.

Kathryn Tann, twenty-three, is from the Vale of Glamorgan and has recently completed her MA in Creative Writing at the University of Manchester. She also has a degree in English Literature from Durham University, and works as a freelancer in publishing. Kathryn writes short fiction and creative non-fiction, and is currently completing her first novel. Her work has appeared in the 2019 Penfro winner's anthology *Heartland*, *The 2020 Manchester Anthology* and *Porridge Magazine*, and she has reviewed literature and theatre for a range of online publications. She also produces and hosts *The Podcast for New Writing* in Manchester. As a writer, Kathryn considers her greatest sources of inspiration to be wild and coastal landscapes, and the wonderful idiosyncrasies of the individual experience.

Thomas Tyrrell lives in Cardiff, where he finished a PhD on John Milton in 2018. He won the poetry prize in *Cheval 10* and *11*, and his piratical poetry pamphlet, *The Poor Rogues Hang,* is published from Mosaique press and available via Amazon and the Waterstones website.

Sidney Wollmuth is currently attending the University of North Carolina Wilmington where she is double-majoring in English Literature and Creative Writing. Her writing has been recognised by the Scholastic Art and Writing competition, *Huffington Post*, *Rookie Mag*, *Pittsburgh Poetry Houses*, and *Sad Girl Review*. She is the Managing Editor of *Atlantis Creative Magazine* (atlantismagazine.org). She loses way too many things.

PARTHIAN   Fiction

Martha, Jack & Shanco

CARYL LEWIS
TRANSLATED BY GWEN DAVIES
ISBN 978-1-912681-77-8
£9.99 • Paperback

Winner of the Wales Book of the Year
"Harsh, lyrical, devastating... sings with a
bitter poetry." – *The Independent*

Love and Other Possibilities

LEWIS DAVIES
ISBN 978-1-906998-08-0
£6.99 • Paperback

Winner of the Rhys Davies Award
"Davies's prose is simple and effortless, the
kind of writing that wins competitions."
– *The Independent*

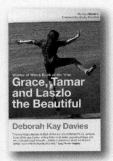

Grace, Tamar and Laszlo the Beautiful

DEBORAH KAY DAVIES
ISBN 978-1-912109-43-2
£8.99 • Paperback

Winner of the Wales Book of the Year
"Davies's writing thrills on all levels."
– Suzy Ceulan Hughes

Hummingbird

TRISTAN HUGHES
ISBN 978-1-91090-90-8
£10 • Hardback
£8.99 • Paperback

Winner of the Stanford Fiction Award
"Superbly accomplished... Hughes's prose is
startling and luminous." – *Financial Times*

PARTHIAN Fiction

The Web of Belonging
Out 2021

STEVIE DAVIES
ISBN 978-1-912681-16-7
£8.99 • Paperback

**"A comic novelist of
the highest order."**
– The Times

The Cormorant
Out 2021

STEPHEN GREGORY
ISBN 978-1-912681-69-3
£8.99 • Paperback

**Winner of the
Somerset Maugham Award**
**"A first-class terror story with a
relentless focus that would have made
Edgar Allan Poe proud."**
– New York Times

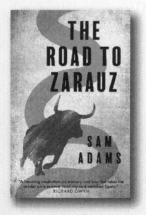

The Road to Zarauz

SAM ADAMS
ISBN 978-1-912681-85-3
£8.99 • Paperback
**"A haunting meditation on memory
and loss that takes the reader on a
summer road trip to a vanished Spain."**
– Richard Gwyn

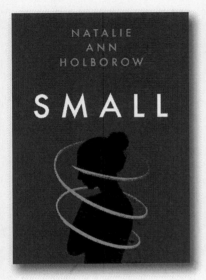